DUSTY AYRES AND HIS BATTLE BIRDS:
THE WHITE DEATH

THE WHITE DEATH

By Robert Sidney Bowen

ALTUS PRESS • 2017

CHAPTER 1
CRAZY ORDERS

BROWS FURROWED in deep thought, Dusty Ayres stared unseeing at the juicy, sizzling steak on the thick aluminum plate in front of him. Across the booth table Curly Brooks was maneuvering a last mouthful onto his fork. He started it toward his lips, but stopped it in mid-air as he noticed his pal.

"Hey, snap it up! Your ice cream's getting cold!"

Dusty looked up and blinked.

"Huh? Oh yeah, sure."

And he made a weak pass at his steak. Curly frowned, and lowered his fork.

"Say, what's the idea?" he grunted. "I thought you were the lad who suggested coming down here to Keene's for a special feed. Why the trance?"

Dusty shrugged.

"Nothing," he said. "I just don't feel so hungry, that's all."

Curly started to speak, but decided to finish the last mouthful. He washed it down with a drink of beer, and cleared his throat.

"Alright, son," he said. "Tell papa all about it. You've been in a sweat for a week, now. Ever since we got back from the Great Circle seadrome show. What in hell is biting you, anyway? You've been acting as though we'd lost the war, or something?"

THE WHITE DEATH

BY ROBERT SIDNEY BOWEN

Dusty's eyes went agate, and his right hand bunched into a hammer-head fist.

"It's that rat!" he grated.

"What rat?" asked Curly. "There's a lot of them on the other side of the Northern front."

Dusty snorted.

"You know who I mean! The Black Hawk. I was positive that we'd nailed him at the Great Circle seadrome. And then we found out that it was only one of his damn pinch-hitters!"

"Well, as Jack Horner said," grunted Brooks. "It's at least one

3

of his pinch-hitters out of the way. You can't expect everything, fellow."

Dusty leaned forward, and his words were like steel against steel.

"I'm going to get him, kid. Get him once and for all—the *real* Black Hawk!"

"Swell idea," nodded Curly. "Now, have some of your steak—it's perfect."

"I mean it!" Dusty persisted. "That tramp is half of the Black Invaders' brains. If I can get him, there's no telling what the results may be. And besides—well, it's getting under my skin. I've fallen down on the job a dozen times, and—"

"Fallen down on the job?" Curly cut in. "Cut the modesty! Hell, Dusty, you've been the Army, Navy and Air Force all wrapped up in one. Why, what about Duluth, and New York, and—"

"Pile it in the next yard!" Dusty got out savagely. "That sort of thing burns me up—and you know it. Luck dropped me into a couple of spectacular shows, but that's not the whole war. And you were with me practically every time, so cut that line. What I mean is that this Black Hawk angle has developed into something personal. It's become a little private war between the two of us. But—here, take a look at this!"

Dusty fished a newspaper flier out of his tunic pocket and tossed it across the table. Curly smoothed it out, and glanced at the printed words. The flier read:

THE WHITE DEATH

WHY?

(Anonymous)

We sincerely admit that Captain Ayres, special emergency air courier by appointment of the President and Congressional Committee, has established himself as the outstanding hero of this terrible and senseless conflict now being waged within our borders. Yet, at the same time, we are forced to analyze in a calm and unbiased manner the net results of this great airman's accomplishments. And we reach the following conclusion:

That Captain Ayres, by dint of great courage and skill, and in cooperation with those closely associated with him, has thwarted several attempts by the enemy to grind us into the ground.

On the surface, it would seem that no one man could do more. Yet, an accounting of these achievements shows that enemy property, rather than enemy personnel, has been destroyed. What of the one known as the Black Hawk—the enemy airman who stands equal with Fire-Eyes in animal cunning, ruthlessness and sheer barbaric savagery? Captain Ayres and the Black Hawk have met on the ground and in the air many times. Yet, always the result seems to be inevitable— the Hawk returns to his fold to prepare new and more dastardly onslaughts against our civilization. And Captain Ayres returns to our fold to receive new honors and new praise that we still quite frankly admit he justly deserves.

But why—why does it always end like that? Have the fates decreed that these two shall go on meeting each other, and parting, both still alive? Or is this Black Hawk some superhuman creature totally immune to the effects of steel bullets in his heart?

We believe neither is the case. And in the interest of a speedy ending to this terrible war, we hope and pray from the bottom of our hearts that the next meeting between these two will terminate in the concrete death of someone—and that some one will be the Black Hawk!

As Curly finished reading he smashed his fist down on the paper.

"Why, the dirty, low down—!"

He stopped short, and glared at the paper again as he turned it over in his hands. It was blank on the other side.

"Who wrote it?" he demanded fiercely. "I'll bust him so hard, he'll bounce for a week!"

"**I DON'T** know," answered Dusty, "Probably one of those anti-war sheets that have been springing up around the country. It's printed as a flier, as you can see. Got one in the mail this morning—postmarked Washington, D.C. I don't imagine that it has appeared in any paper. Somehow, I don't think they'd dare to."

"They'd better not!" gritted Curly. Then in softer tone, "But you're not letting this get you, kid? You know it isn't true. Hell, everyone knows it isn't true!"

Dusty didn't answer for a long minute. He sat staring at Brooks without actually seeing him.

"I don't know about that, Curly," he said eventually. "There is something in what he says. We have busted up a lot of Black Invader war property—but we haven't done so good as regards reducing man-power. And that's what will win this war, eventually—smashing down man-power."

"Granted," Curly nodded. "But what the hell do you think the public expects you, or anyone else, to do—walk into Invader territory and smack down Fire-Eyes, the Hawk and the rest of their tramp officers, just like that?"

Dusty reached out and tapped the flier.

" 'Anonymous' does!"

Brooks cursed.

"The hell with what he thinks!" he snarled. "Let him take a crack at it, and see for himself!"

Dusty shook his head.

"Nope! Me first!"

Curly gulped down the last of his beer and slammed the mug down on the table so hard that the handle snapped off.

"Sometimes I really think you are screwy!" he growled. "Come on, let's get the hell back to the field. And just for that dumb talk you've been shooting off, you can settle the check!"

Heaving himself to his feet, Brooks slapped his service cap on the side of his head and stamped out of the chop house. Dusty, a faint grin tugging at the corners of his mouth, paid the check at the cashier's cage and followed him out. Curly was already behind the wheel of the Group car they'd borrowed for the trip in town and he was glaring straight ahead. Dusty got in and slouched back against the cushions.

"The Hawk's home drome, James," he chuckled. "And quickly, please!"

Curly meshed gears savagely and shot him a sidelong glance.

"So help me, Dusty!" he snapped. "I mean it! If you try to carry out that screwy idea that's buzzing around inside your dome, I'll yank you back and tie you to your hutment bunk—and I don't mean perhaps, either!"

"Oh well, that's that, then," said Dusty with a mocking sigh. "You always did make me tremble inside."

Brooks started to speak again. Then checked himself and snapped his lips shut. He knew Dusty too well to try to argue him out of any idea once it took root in his brain. And so, lean face set in grim determination, he sent the Group car rocketing along the state highway that led to the home drome of High Speed Group 7.

Half an hour later he skidded it to a halt on the tarmac, and turned to his pal.

"How about a long one, with plenty of ice in it?" he asked casually.

Dusty grinned.

"Want to stick close, eh?" he chuckled. "O.K. I'm not leaving yet. Got to dope out a few things, first. Lead the way, my stubborn protector."

But Curly didn't. As they were climbing out of the car a Group office orderly came running up. He clicked his heels in front of Dusty and saluted.

"Major Drake wants to see you, sir."

"Right," Dusty nodded. Then to Curly, "Fix me up one, kid. I'll join you in the mess in a couple of minutes."

TURNING ON his heel he swung down the tarmac and in

through the Group office door. The C.O., parked behind his big desk, glanced up as he entered.

"Have a chair, Ayres," he grunted. And then as Dusty seated himself, "You've seen one of them, I suppose?"

"Seen one of what?"

Major Drake pushed one of the fliers across the desk. Dusty glanced at it and nodded.

"Yeah. Some bright lad sent me one through the mail, yesterday."

"And your reaction?" asked the C.O. softly.

Dusty looked him square in the eye.

"What do you think, sir?"

The other shook his head sadly.

"I was afraid of that, knowing you," he said. "But, listen, it's no soap. You're grounded."

Dusty came off his chair like a streak of light.

"I'm what?" he roared savagely.

Major Drake waved him back.

"Grounded, Ayres," he said. "Spelled g-r-o-u-n-d-e-d, grounded! And this makes it stick!"

He pulled a radiogram out from under the blotter and held it out. Dusty grabbed it and glared at the printed message.

Major Brake,
H.S. Group 7
Captain Ayres is to be grounded until further orders.
(Signed) Bradley.

"But he can't do that!" Dusty shouted, as he hurled the radiogram back on the desk. "I don't give a hoot if he is chief of air force staff! He—"

"Hold it! Keep your shirt on!"

The words came off Major Drake's lips like machine-gun bullets. Dusty swallowed hard, and slumped down on his chair.

"Sorry, major," he grunted. "Guess I went off half-cocked. But that damn newspaper flier—"

"Seems to be doing exactly what it was intended to do!" the C.O. finished sharply. "Hell, do you think that lying bunch of tripe is common belief?"

Dusty shrugged stubbornly.

"Maybe yes, maybe no," he got out in a flat tone. "But, it has its points. We could do swell without the Hawk!"

Major Drake sighed.

"You're quite right," he said. "But look at it this way—who did the Black Invaders declare war against?"

"Huh? I don't think I get you."

"Then I'll explain. War was declared against the people of these United States—not against just one person!"

Dusty flushed slightly.

"I get it," he said. "Guess I was thinking more of my own feelings. But that grounding order—"

"Was the first one I received," the C.O. cut him off. "This came half an hour ago."

He took a second radiogram from under the blotter and handed it out. Dusty held his breath as he reached for it. It read:

Major Drake,

H.S. Group 7

You will instruct Captain Ayres to proceed to Washington H.Q. by Staff train 567 leaving Springfield 2:25. Captain Ayres is to be provided with escort to station and placed in custody of Staff Sergeant Bolton in Car Four. Sergeant Bolton will be supplied with a duplicate of this order.

Signed, Bradley.

Dusty read it through twice, then raised questioning eyes to Major Drake's face. "And now, what do you suppose?" he murmured dully.

The C.O. shrugged.

"Most anything," he said. "As I've told you many times before, Washington H.Q. loves to be secretive about everything. However, perhaps they're justified. Frankly, though, I wish this second order hadn't come through."

Dusty's eyebrows went up in surprise.

"And why?"

Major Drake stared thoughtfully out the window.

"For your sake," he said with feeling. "I'm afraid that Washington H.Q. is getting to believe that you really are a miracle man—you've pulled off so many damn fine things. And—well, I don't want to see them ask you to do one stunt too many, that's all."

Dusty's heart pounded against his ribs. He'd known Major Drake for years—always liked him, and believed that the grizzly old C.O. liked him. But, up until now, he never dreamed that the affection was that deep. He leaned forward and grinned.

"Thanks, sir," he said. "But don't worry—if it works out so that I can get another real good crack at the Hawk, I'll be the happiest guy alive. After all, sir, as you say—it isn't a war against one man. And I'm just one of millions who at least *try* to carry out orders."

The C.O. didn't miss the emphasis on the single word. He smiled faintly and nodded.

"Yes, you at least start out to obey orders," he said. "But fate usually puts you on your own before you've gone very far. And—oh hell, why try to talk to you about it. Better get ready now. I'll have a car and escort for you in twenty minutes. As usual—luck, son!"

Once outside the Group office Dusty started to hotfoot it over to his hutment. But as he went past the mess lounge door Curly confronted him.

"Slow down for a curve," he said. "Do you want this drink, or not?"

"Have it yourself, sweetheart," Dusty called back over his shoulder. "I've got things to do just now."

Brooks cursed and raced after him.

"Now you listen to me, dumb-bell!" he panted. "I'm not going to—"

"Save it, kid," Dusty cut him off, ducking into his hutment. "It's not what you think. Ordered to Washington—by train."

"By *what?*" yelped Curly as the door slammed in his face.

He waited and repeated the question when Dusty reappeared fifteen minutes later. His pal nodded.

DUSTY AYRES

"Yeah, by train," he said. "Escort to a Staff train waiting at the Springfield station. Orders from Bradley."

"But what the hell's up?" persisted Brooks as they started over to where the Group car and two motorcycle guards were waiting. "Haven't you any idea?"

Dusty tossed his kit-bag onto the back seat, and climbed in after it.

"Not the slightest," he grinned at Curly. "I've only got hopes."

Brooks frowned, stepped close and laid a hand on Dusty's arm.

"A promise, fellow," he said in deadly seriousness, "if you can possibly make it a two-man job—make it that way, will you?"

Dusty chuckled.

"As if I could go any place without my shadow!" he said. "Hell yes, Curly, of course it's a promise. O.K., corporal, let her out!"

The non-com behind the wheel meshed gears and the car moved forward flanked on either side by a motorcycle guard. Turning in the seat, Dusty flung Curly a kidding thumb-to-the-nose salute. Brooks returned it with a couple of additional gestures.

And the two of them little dreamed of the hell fires that would sweep across the earth before their next meeting.

CHAPTER 2
DEATH ON WHEELS

S LUMPED BACK against the rear-seat cushions Dusty stared absently at the back of the driver's head and took stock of the situation up to the present. The net result was indeed small, and absolutely unenlightening.

Bradley wanted him at Washington H.Q., and wanted him to travel by Staff train. Why? The answer—damned if he knew. Another question—was there any tie-up between Bradley's order and that damn newspaper flier? Answer—maybe yes, maybe no. He'd find that out later.

Impulsively he jammed a hand in his tunic pocket and pulled out his crumpled copy. He read it through for the umpteenth time; rammed it back in his pocket again.

"Curly's right," he grunted. "So's the major. I shouldn't let this thing get me. But dammit, I'm human, the same as anyone else! I don't like ribbing. Not this kind, anyway. By God, I'll get that—"

He let the rest fade out as the mighty thunder of airplane engines came to him from high up and off to the right. Turning in that direction he shielded his eyes against the sun's glare and stared heavenward.

A moment later he saw them—a full squadron of low-wing, twin-engined Yank bombers. In perfect raid formation they were roaring toward the north and the war. He grinned and snapped a salute.

"Give 'em hell, boys," he said. "And lay a couple for me!"

15

Eyes still on the ships he watched them thunder over Springfield, directly ahead, and continue on up through the heart of Massachusetts, each ship gaining altitude with every rev of its twin props.

And then without warning it happened.

The last line of the giant aerial armada was sweeping up into a great cloud bank when, suddenly, the cloud bank appeared to burst apart in a terrific flash of dazzling white light. At the same instant there was a crashing roar of sound. It was as though the very heavens themselves had been split asunder.

Impulsively, Dusty leaped to his feet, yelled to the driver to stop, and stood braced against the front seat, eyes glued upward. The northern heavens were now a great conglomerate expanse of sizzling balls of white light that zipped and darted about in all directions.

As a matter of fact, they looked like so many crazy white comets brilliantly silhouetted against a background of oily black smoke and crimson flame.

"Good lord—look! That plane, to the right—it's one of the bombers!"

The driver's cry fell on deaf ears as far as Dusty was concerned. He was already staring wide-eyed at the weird and eerie phenomenon high up in the air.

One of the bombers was slowly fluttering down like some giant broken-winged bird. But, it was not that fact alone that caused little fingers of ice to clutch at Dusty's heart. The bomber was in reality only the framework skeleton of a bomber.

There seemed to be no metal covering over the wings, the

guns and bomb turrets, or the main fuselage. Instead, everything was shrouded by a pale yet sparkling phosphorescent glow that made the framework stand out, just as the bones of the human body stand out in an X-ray picture.

And as the great craft swooped lower and lower it left behind a wide trail of shooting sparks.

"There must be covering! Hell, it would drop like a rock!" DUSTY'S OWN words echoed back to him from miles away. Like a man in a trance he stood watching the horrible sight to the north.

One by one a dozen or more of the bombers came fluttering or spinning earthward. Some were but smoking balls of flame, but at least three of them were sparkle-shrouded framework.

Perhaps it was five minutes—it seemed like five years—before there was nothing left in the air save floating smoke and drifting clouds. Every bomber had disappeared down over the rim of the horizon.

Face drawn and muscles taut Dusty sank back on the seat. It was then that he first noticed the non-com driver and the two motorcycle guards. They were looking at him out of eyes brimming with awe, eerie wonder, and fear. It was sudden realization that perhaps his own expression reflected theirs that made him snap out of his trance. He motioned them into action.

"The station!" he snapped. "Hellbent!"

They needed no further urging. The motorcycle escort clattered down the road, and the car roared after it. In less than no time it slithered to a stop in front of the station. An armed guard jumped forward and jerked open the door.

"Captain Ayres?"

"Right," Dusty nodded.

"This way, sir," said the guard. "Colonel Parks is waiting for you in the Transport office."

Dusty didn't have the slightest idea who Colonel Parks might be, but he found out about two minutes later when the guard ushered him into his office. The colonel was military rolling-stock dispatcher for the area. He was also, short, fat, and in a highly nervous condition as Dusty introduced himself.

"Take a chair, Captain Ayres," he babbled out. "Yes, by all means take a chair. I've a radiogram instructing you to wait here for further orders. God, captain—did you see those bombers? They tell me they all exploded. Good Lord, that's horrible—horrible, captain!"

Dusty nodded shortly, put out his hand.

"May I see that radiogram, sir?" he asked.

"Eh?" the other gaped at him. "Radiogram? Oh yes, yes! Here you are, captain. God, those poor devils in those bombers! To think that—"

Dusty didn't bother listening to what Colonel Parks thought. He took the radiogram from his trembling fingers and smoothed it out. It was to Parks from General Bradley, and read:

> Hold Captain Ayres at Springfield Station until further orders.

Just those nine words and nothing more. Dusty scowled at it, snapped his free thumb against it, then dropped it on Parks' desk. The military dispatcher was still jabbering about the bombers, but Dusty still refused to listen.

The old familiar feeling was surging through him. It was the feeling, rather the inner sensation, that he had experienced countless times since the outbreak of war. In short, something was haywire. There was mystery hanging around—too damn much mystery, that didn't even add up to a little sense.

He fumed over it for a couple of minutes, then faced Colonel Parks.

"Mind if I use your Teletype, sir?" he asked, pointing to the instrument on a corner table.

"Eh? Teletype? Why—what for, captain?"

"I want to check with General Bradley," Dusty told him bluntly.

The transport officer stared at him in surprise.

"But there is nothing to check, captain!" he protested. "That order came through over an hour ago."

Dusty, who was already seating himself at the keyboard, suddenly whirled.

"What? What's that?" he demanded, and shot out a finger at the radiogram. "You got that over an hour ago? What was the exact time?"

Colonel Parks squinted at the form.

"Twelve-fifty-five," he said. "Yes, that's what it says right here, see? As a matter of fact, I wondered a bit myself. It came through not more than five minutes after the order to hold Staff train Five-Sixty-Seven for your arrival."

Dusty scowled hard at the opposite wall.

"Hum-m-m!" he murmured. Then aloud to himself, "Orders for me to wait here coming through before Drake got orders for me to leave? Now what the hell? Why the delay?"

"Eh?" gaped Parks. "What's that you say, captain?"

The pilot ignored him, seated himself at the Teletype machine again, and snapped on power. He waited a moment for the coils to warm up, then started punching out the message:

Ayres to Bradley, Washington H.Q.
Waiting at Springfield. Request reason for departure delay.
Suggest trip be made by air at once.

Sitting back he glued his eyes on the glass-domed roll of ticker tape. A minute dragged by, and then the tape wheel started clicking over, and words appeared on the tape.

Bradley to Ayres, Springfield.
Embark Washington at once on Staff train 567.

Dusty ripped off the strip of tape and handed it to Colonel Parks.

"There's my orders, sir," he said getting up. "I'm leaving now. What track's it on?"

"Seven," the other answered promptly for the first time. "Come along, captain, I'll see that you get aboard."

CATCHING UP his kit-bag Dusty followed him out of the office and down the long concrete ramp leading to the train level. The train was a three-car streamlined affair, but as Dusty swept it with his eyes he noted that there was no car number

4. He mentioned the fact to Parks and the transport officer gulped.

"Good lord!" he gapped. "I'm sure I told the yard chief to include number 4 in this hook-up. It's a combination engine and club car. Oh well, it doesn't matter. Come along, captain, I'll see that you get a compartment in number 9 here at the end. As a matter of fact, I prefer a rear car myself."

With a shrug, Dusty followed him down the platform and into an empty compartment in car number 9. Parks fussed about for a couple of minutes, patting this cushion and that cushion, and eased his fat figure down onto the platform again.

"A pleasant journey, captain," he beamed. "And I hope we meet again sometime real soon. It has been a joy, making your acquaintance."

Dusty nodded, and said, "Thanks, colonel. I hope we do meet again soon."

At that moment the starter's whistle shrilled along the platform and a quiver of power went through the train. Leaning forward Dusty pulled the compartment door shut, and in practically the same motion snapped Colonel Parks a salute. Whether the transport officer returned the salute, he didn't know, because the train moved forward and the short, fat man was lost to view.

Unloosening his tunic, Dusty slouched back against the cushions, fished a cigarette from his pocket and lighted up. The train was now racing through the tunnel under the city of Springfield, and the automatic lights in the compartment were burning brightly.

As Dusty glanced at them, they suddenly reminded him of the shooting white comets about those doomed bombers, and he unconsciously stiffened in the seat.

"Damn!" he breathed. "Should have found out more about them. They went down close to the city. Wonder if the gang highballed up there? Perhaps—"

His voice trailed off, but his thoughts continued. And to say the least, they were not pleasant thoughts. Nothing that had happened during the last four hours made any sense. And it still didn't make sense half an hour later, when a thin-faced sergeant appeared at the inside corridor door, jerked it open and saluted smartly.

"Captain Ayres?"

Dusty nodded.

"And you, sergeant?" he asked.

"Sergeant Bolton, sir," replied the other. "I'm detailed to you."

"Then come in and sit down, sergeant," smiled Dusty. "Have a cigarette?"

The non-com seemed not to see the pack he held out.

"Your compartment is in the forward car, sir," he said. "In number 4."

Dusty shrugged.

"This is as good as any, sergeant," he said. "Besides, the head car isn't number 4. There was a slip-up, and it wasn't hooked onto the train."

"I think you must be mistaken, sir," was the startling remark from the non-com. "It's number 4 alright. And your compartment's waiting for you."

As the man spoke, an eerie warning of impending danger sounded inside Dusty's head. He stared hard at the sergeant, and noticed for the first time that the man was out of breath, and striving his best to conceal the fact. In other words, he had all the appearances of a man who had been dashing frantically through the train in search of some one.

With calm deliberation, yet watching the sergeant every second, Dusty pulled a fresh cigarette from his park and lighted from the glowing stub of his first. He spilled smoke ceilingward and settled back more comfortably against the cushions.

"Sit down and tell me all about it, sergeant," he said quietly. "The lead car is *not* number 4. But, assuming that it is, why isn't this compartment just as good?"

The non-com licked his lips and shrugged helplessly.

"Orders, sir," he said. "I was told to put you in car number 4. That's—that's the car General Bradley will take at New York, sir."

Dusty's eyes widened in surprise.

"General Bradley is in New York?" he asked casually.

The other nodded.

"Yes, sir," he said promptly. "I believe he's waiting for you there, now."

Dusty nodded, and snubbed out his half-smoked cigarette. Getting to his feet he started to button up his tunic.

"Well, in that case," he grunted, adjusting his Sam Browne, "I guess I'd better go up to car 4. If—"

HE FINISHED the rest with lightning-like movement, not

words. Faster than the eye could follow his hand swept down and came up gripping his service automatic.

He rammed the muzzle against the sergeant's stomach, and with his other hand grabbed him by the slack front of his tunic and jerked him into the compartment. A quick twist and the man went spinning down onto the compartment seat. Bending over, Dusty jerked the other's gun from its holster and shoved it in his pocket. Then he spoke.

"Okay, rat, the show's over! And you certainly take first prize for bum acting!"

The non-com gaped at him out of dumbfounded eyes.

"But sir," he gulped out. "What do you mean? What is the idea, sir?"

Eyes agate, Dusty clipped him across the side of the face with his gun barrel. The man yelped and put a hand to his cheek.

"I was almost beginning to believe you," Dusty grated at him. "And then you pulled the prize boner. General Bradley isn't in New York, sweetheart. You see, I happen to know that little fact."

"But I thought he was, sir," the other moaned. "That's what I understood, sir."

"You did, like hell!" Dusty cracked at him. "What happened to car 4?"

"It's the first car on this train!" the sergeant wailed. "Go up there, sir. Go up and see for yourself."

"I still like this place," grunted Dusty. And with face granite, he gun-whipped the man again. "Spit it out!" he snapped. "Where's the Hawk? You got your orders from him, didn't you?"

"I don't know what you're talking about!" the other whined. "What Hawk? Who's the Hawk?"

Dusty's lips came together in a thin line, and his eyes blazed up.

"Mistake, number two, rat!" he said softly. "There isn't a Yank soldier who doesn't know of the Hawk. You slipped, that time. Now, let's have the whole story. What's this all about? Why are you here?"

The other hesitated, seemed to brace himself.

"But I told you, sir, that—"

He finished the rest with a howl of pain, as Dusty's gun barrel cut him across the right cheek.

"And more coming up!" Dusty hurled at him. "More coming up, unless you start talking."

The sergeant cringed back against the cushions, but into his eyes seeped a light of stark hatred. It was a sort of Dr. Jekyll-Mr. Hyde transformation. His thin face seemed to get even thinner, giving the whole a vulture-like appearance. Dusty stared down into it, a hard smile on his lips.

"The sign of the breed comes to the surface, eventually, eh?" he grunted. "Okay! Start talking."

"There is nothing for my lips to say!" snarled the man. "I know nothing. And I do not fear death. Do as you wish, you dog. But, mine will be the last laugh—you will never leave this train alive!"

Dusty grinned.

"Just like that? Well, I haven't got time to beat the truth out of you. So, will just turn you over to some one who will."

HOLD IT!
HE BARKED—

26

As he spoke the words he reached out his free hand and jabbed the button that would signal the engineer up ahead to stop the train. Holding his thumb against it, he still continued to grin at the man.

But as the seconds flew past the train did not stop. In fact, it didn't even slow down at all. Dusty's face must have expressed the chagrin that he felt, for the sergeant laughed harshly.

"Fool! Did you not think I was prepared?" he hissed. "Look there—the contact switch has been broken. That button you push signals no one!"

Impulsively, Dusty whirled to glance at the contact switch. And as he did, the sergeant hurled himself toward the open compartment door. But, in doing so he signed his own death warrant. Dusty's gun snapped up and around.

"Hold it!" he barked.

The sergeant refused. He plunged forward through the door. A split second later Dusty's gun smashed out flame and sound. The sergeant cried out, wheeled around, arched over backwards and clawed at the compartment door jamb as he slid to the floor. Glassy eyes found Dusty's face. Blood-flecked lips twitched, and hissing words slid out from between them.

"You will die—it has been so written—you—will die—!"

The hissing voice trailed off into silence, and the man died.

Face expressionless, Dusty stared down at him, then stepped over the lifeless body and out into the corridor. There he paused, looked down at the man again. "You asked for it," he said softly, "and you got it!"

Turning toward the forward end of the train, he stooped over a minute, and glanced out the window. The train was rushing past a large wood. He wasn't sure, but he judged it to be some part of lower Connecticut, near the New York line. Straightening up, he started along the corridor forward. As he passed each compartment he glanced inside. All were empty.

He entered the second car and discovered the same thing. Unless there were people in the forward car, he was alone on the train. A scowl furrowing his brows, he started toward the lead car; the one that contained the powerplant of the train.

And when he was a couple of dozen steps from the front vestibule door of the second car—it happened!

There was a terrific scream of sound. It was like a high-speed rotary saw ripping and tearing through sheet metal. And at the same instant everything was blotted out by a great flash of shimmering white light.

For the tiniest fraction of a second, Dusty had the vision of a wavy ribbon of white slithering down past the car windows and into the ground. And then, he was hurled headlong onto the floor. Hardly had he touched it, before he was jerked up and thrown through a compartment door.

And after that, until a great cloud of inky darkness engulfed him, everything was but a spinning, whirling conglomeration of crashing sound, brilliant light, and violent topsy-turvy movement.

CHAPTER 3
THE DOOR TO HELL

"**H**EY!—STRETCHER BEARERS,** this way! There's an officer in here! Snap it up, damn you!"

"Say—who do you think you are? Ain't I coming as fast as I can?"

Words! Words coming from the lips of two different persons. Floating about in a great white fog, Dusty heard them. But, where in hell did they come from? He couldn't see a thing. Not a single thing except limitless space shrouded with clinging fog. And in the center of the fog there was a spot of fused light. Almost like the sun trying to burn through dawn ground mist.

"Easy there! Don't give it to him all at once, you dummy!"

A voice again! Something was burning his throat. Liquid fire was pouring down his throat. His whole chest seemed in flames.

And then, suddenly, the fused light in the fog grew bigger and bigger. And presently there was no more fog, and his half-conscious brain told him that his eyes were staring at blurred objects—objects that were moving.

Finally, they cleared, took on definite shape and outline, and he saw the head and shoulders of two uniformed men bending over him. One wore Staff sergeant insignia. The other, that of the Medical Corps.

The lips of the Staff sergeant moved, and words penetrated Dusty's dulled brain.

"Are you hurt bad, sir?"

In an abstract sort of way Dusty's brain toyed with the question. Hurt bad? Who was hurt bad? Him? But, why? What the hell had happened?

Around and around raced the questions, and then, suddenly, like flood-waters spilled through the broken dam, memory rushed back to him. He was hardly conscious of his own voice as he shouted the words.

"The train! Yeah—something happened to the train! It must have been wrecked."

"Take it easy, sir. Here, have a bit more of this."

The Staff sergeant held a flask to his lips, and more liquid fire went down his throat. It gagged him. He coughed hoarsely and pushed the flask away. But it accomplished its purpose. His brain cleared, and a dull aching at the back of his head faded away.

It was then that he realized that he was propped up against a tree trunk. One of his field boots was missing, and the other breeches leg was torn to shreds. The top part of his uniform was in good condition, save for a few grease smudges here and there.

He raised his eyes to the two soldiers bending over him, and gasped aloud. It was not because of them that he gasped, but because of what he saw as his eyes looked past them.

Fifty yards away was the streamlined Staff train, a twisted and crumpled mass of dural and steel that was slumped over on its side in the drainage ditch that paralleled both sides of the four-way tracks.

The two end cars still retained some of their original shape.

But the front car was little more than a flame-charred strip of melted junk. From one end to the other it was streaked with black, and the trucks, upon which it had once rested, had been hopelessly twisted and warped out of line.

In fact, as Dusty stared at it, he had the crazy sensation that the forward car had plunged right into the very heart of a blast furnace. Frowning, he switched his eyes to the Staff sergeant's face.

"You saw?—you saw what happened? Did we hit something?"

The non-com shook his head.

"No sir," he said. "Something—something hit you. It looked like ribbon lightning, sir."

Impulsively, Dusty raised his eyes heavenward. The sun was blazing down out of a limitless expanse of blue. There wasn't a cloud to be seen within the boundaries of the four horizons.

"Ribbon lightning?" he echoed, snapping his eyes back to the non-com. "Are you trying to kid me?"

"NO SIR," the man answered instantly. "My God, no! I was trying to catch you. Trying to signal the engineer to stop, when—well a long ribbon of something white suddenly shot down and struck the lead car. It melted right then and there, sir, so help me God! And the other two cars went slamming off the rails. I radioed the nearest medical unit, then landed in the field over there. We found you jammed under the seat in one of the compartments of the second car. And we found a sergeant, too, in the rear car. He—he was in two pieces."

Dusty let the man talk until he stopped voluntarily. Then he fixed him with a steady look.

"Trying to catch me?" he asked. "Start at the beginning, and give me the whole story. Just why were you trying to catch me?"

"You're Captain Ayres, aren't you, sir?" the non-com shot back at him.

"Right the first time," Dusty nodded. "Go ahead."

The other paused a minute, as though he were at loss as just how to begin.

"Well, it was like this, sir," he suddenly blurted out. "I received orders from Springfield Area Staff this noon to act as escort detail on train 567. And I was told that I was to ride with you in car 4. And—"

"Then you're Sergeant Bolton?" Dusty cut in.

"Yes sir," the man nodded. "Rank of sergeant pilot and attached to Springfield Staff for courier work. Well, as I started to say, after I was appointed detail, I went to the station yards to check car number 4. There was a couple of porters fixing the car up. I stopped to talk with one of them, and—"

The non-com paused, and looked sheepish.

"And what?" Dusty encouraged.

"Well, that was the last thing I knew, until I woke up. I think I was slugged. Anyway, there was a goose egg on the top of my head. Well, I hot-footed it to the station, and found out from Colonel Parks that your train had left. That gave me a hunch that something was going wrong."

"A damn good hunch, too, sergeant!" Dusty grunted grimly.

"Yes sir," the non-com nodded. "And—well, I hope you'll understand me, sir, but—but Colonel Parks got kind of rattled, if you know what I mean. So without asking his permission I

teletyped to the train, but couldn't get any answer. So I wired to Stamford to flag you down, and tore out to Staff field. Maybe I shouldn't have done that, sir, but you see I kinda had the feeling that I was responsible for anything that might happen. Well, anyway, I grabbed the first ship I saw, and came highballing after you. And—well, it's like I was just telling you. There was a long flash of ribbon lightning, and that lead car just melted into the tracks."

The non-com stopped and sucked in a deep breath. Dusty stared at the wrecked train, and an eerie tingle rippled up and down his spine.

"So that's why the rat wanted me in the lead car?" he murmured aloud.

"Huh? Someone tried to get you into it, sir?" spoke up the Staff sergeant.

"Yeah," Dusty nodded. "That man you found in two pieces. He is—or was—a Black agent. And a dumb one, too. But, tell me—you didn't see anything except that ribbon lightning? Where did it come from? What direction, I mean?"

The non-com looked sheepish again.

"Far as I know, sir, it came straight down from above. Another minute and it would have hit me. I guess—well I guess that the train folding up, the way it did, knocked me for such a loop that I was too surprised to do anything except stare at the train. It was a pretty awful sight, sir. Later, I did look around, but I didn't see anything, sir."

"Did you see those bombers go down?" Dusty suddenly asked him. "The ones north of Springfield?"

The sergeant shook his head.

"No sir, I didn't," he said. "But I heard them. My guess is that

34

a load of Tetalyne aboard one of them, went off by mistake, and set off the others along with it."

Dusty got slowly to his feet, tested his weight on his legs, and found that save for a slight stiffness in the right knee that he was in fair-to-middling shape.

THE STAFF sergeant and the medical man straightened up also, and stood silently staring at him. He ignored them for a minute or two, and stared hard across the Connecticut countryside. Presently he shot out a finger at Bolton.

"Your orders about train escort detail? Who did they come from?"

"Why, Colonel Travers, Springfield Area Staff C.O., sir," was the prompt answer.

Dusty gestured with his hand.

"No, I don't mean that," he said. "I mean, do you know who originally sent out the order? Was it sent out from Washington?"

Bolton nodded vigorously.

"Oh yes, sir," he said. "Colonel Travers told me he had received it, about eleven-thirty from General Bradley. He told me that so I'd be sure to stick close to the job—it would be that important."

"I see," grunted Dusty. "Now one more question. Did that order to hold me at the station come through Springfield Area Staff, too?"

"What's that, sir?" echoed Bolton his eyes puzzled. "An order holding you at the station? There wasn't any order like that to my knowledge."

"Direct to Sparks, eh?" murmured Dusty to himself. "Yeah, they would work it that way."

Then in louder tone to Bolton:

"Where did you say your ship was, sergeant? I want to borrow it to barge down to Washington H.Q. I think this thing starts to untangle from that point."

The non-com pointed to the left.

"Just beyond this hill, sir," he said.

"Good," nodded Dusty turning away. "Thanks for everything, you two. I'll see that you're not forgotten—particularly you, sergeant."

Bolton ran after him and touched his arm.

"Pardon, sir," he said, "but—well, the ship's a cabin job, and you've had quite a bump. I'd—I'd like to fly you down, sir, if you don't mind."

Dusty didn't miss the pleading eagerness in the man's face. He hesitated a moment then nodded.

"Someone's got to take the ship back," he said. "So come along, sergeant. But, you're the passenger. Always like to handle the stick myself. Funny that way."

"Sure, sir, sure!" beamed the non-com. "I understand, and thanks, sir."

It was less than a four-minute walk over the brow of the hill and down into the two-by-four field where rested a sleek center-wing cabin job with Staff markings. So small was the field that Dusty shot a look of admiration at the non-com. It took a real pilot to sit down in that small space.

"You rate more than courier work, sergeant," he grinned,

climbing in through the small cabin door. "I know plenty of lads who would overshoot this field."

"Darn near did it myself," replied Bolton, striving to keep his voice casual, and failing utterly. "Just lucky I guess."

Dusty made no comment. He busied himself with booting the engine into life, and wheel-braking around into the wind. But at the same time his instinctive liking for Bolton went up a couple of notches. And he made a mental note to recommend the non-com for work more in keeping with his flying ability than behind-the-Front courier work.

Pausing a few seconds to check the instruments, he fed hop to the cowled engine in the nose and lifted the plane clear in less than a twenty-yard run. Holding the nose up, he swung around to the south, and glanced back down at the wrecked train.

It was a gruesome sight indeed, and in spite of himself, a cold shiver ran through him. Just one minute more and he would have entered the lead car. One minute—the time limit between life and death.

Impulsively he jerked his gaze upward and studied the heavens. Off to the west he spotted a flight of Yank planes. They were evidently out on formation practice patrol, for they were making no movement toward the north. But, apart from them, the heavens were empty of ships.

When twenty thousand was reached he leveled off and reached out his free hand to call Washington H.Q. on the radio. But even as he touched the wave-length dial knob, the red signal light on the panel blinked rapidly. A glance at the dial told him that some station was broadcasting on S.O.S. Emergency.

It took him a matter of a split second to snap on full reception volume and contact the proper wave-length. Instantly the speaker unit on the cabin wall rattled out crisp words.

"...Twentieth Bombers! Calling Twentieth Bombers! Check back immediately on S.O.S. Emergency Ten-Eight Six! Calling Twentieth Bombers. B Flight—B Flight—report at once what happened. Calling B Flight, Twentieth Bombers. S.O.S. Emergency!"

The speaker unit clicked silent. Body tense, Dusty glued his eyes to the unit, and waited for the check-back signals. Seconds dragged past and became a minute. Then two minutes—and three minutes.

The speaker unit crackled words again. But it was the same station calling the Twentieth Bombers. As it went silent once more, Dusty sensed rather than saw Sergeant Bolton at his shoulder. The non-com was breathing hoarsely.

"Gosh! That must have been that outfit that—"

DUSTY CUT him off with a savage gesture. Sound was beginning to come out of the speaker unit—sound so faint, that it was little more than a whisper. With a quick movement Dusty moved the volume control needle up against the last peg, but the result was practically negligible. The sounds that continued to come forth from the speaker unit were still so faint and blurred together that they meant nothing at all.

And then, suddenly, without warning, they blared up to almost a roar.

"—down at C Fifty-six! Trapped by—Send warning that Blacks have—"

A sharp click in the speaker unit and it went silent again. A moment later it rattled out frantic calls from the original broadcasting station. But, it was all a waste of words. The calls were repeated five times in the space of three minutes, but not even a murmuring check-back came through. And then the original station went off the air.

Oblivious to the excited mumble of words spilling off Sergeant Bolton's lips, Dusty bent forward and checked the station directional-finder needle and the roller map. What he discovered brought his brows together in a heavy frown. The original station was located about three hundred miles west of his present position. And according to the roller map it must be the main station of the Northeastern Area Bombing H.Q. at Pittsburgh.

"What the hell?" he grunted aloud.

"What sir?" came Bolton's voice at his elbow. "What's the matter?"

Dusty pointed at the directional-finder dial, and then at the roller map.

"See that?" he said. "Now, why the hell should bombers leaving Pittsburgh go way the hell east of Springfield before heading up toward the Front? That's wasting gasoline on a triangular course. They should have cut right straight up through New York State. And—wait a minute."

Spinning the wave-length dial he grabbed up the transmitter tube.

"Calling N.E. Bomber H.Q. on six-nine-seven!" he snapped

out. "Captain Ayres calling N.E. Bomber H.Q. on six-nine-seven!"

Thirty seconds after he stopped calling, the speaker unit crackled on the check-back.

"On your wave-length. Go ahead!"

Dusty hesitated, then put his lips to the transmitter tube.

"Can you tell me original objective of bomber squadron destroyed north of Springfield this noon?" he asked.

There was a moment of silence, then the speaker unit gave forth sound.

"Sorry, but we can't. Objective was secret. However, bombers should not have come within two hundred miles of city named. Can you give us any information?"

Dusty unconsciously shook his head, as though the owner of the voice was standing right in front of him.

"Nothing that you don't know already," he called back. "I saw bombers go down, but have no explanation. Will call you if I find out anything. Signing off."

Flipping the switch down, Dusty leaned back and stared hard straight in front of him.

"What's it all about, sir?" asked Bolton. "I don't get it at all. What made them ships pass over Springfield? And that crazy message we cut in on—where's C Fifty-six? I—cripes, that's a Black territory map position reading, isn't it?"

Dusty nodded absently.

"Yeah," he said. "C Fifty-six is about two hundred miles northwest of Montreal. Don't forget that, sergeant—C Fifty-six!"

"Huh? Why, sir?"

Dusty slanted the ship down in a long racing dive toward the Nation's capital that was looming up over the southern horizon.

"Because it may come in handy, if we draw nothing but blanks down here," he said.

Ten minutes later he coasted the ship in over the Washington military field, sliced down on wingtip and fish-tailed to a perfect three point right smack on the tarmac. Legging out, he turned and grabbed Bolton by the arm.

"Rustle up a car, quick!" he snapped. "I'll meet you at the field office in two minutes."

BOLTON DIDN'T even take time to either nod or salute. He went bounding off toward the motor park. And as he left, Dusty swung around and ran down the tarmac to the field office. As he barged inside, a lean major seated behind the desk jerked up startled eyes.

"Sorry, major," Dusty smiled reaching for the phone. "I want to use this."

The major started to bark out words but checked himself as he recognized his whirlwind visitor.

"Er—yes! Go right ahead, Captain Ayres."

Dusty dialed a number, and waited a few seconds for contact to be made.

"Air Force H.Q.?" he asked when a voice came on the other end. "Captain Ayres speaking. Put me through to General Bradley's office, pronto."

"Sorry, captain," said the voice at the other end, "but, the general is in conference. And orders are not to disturb him."

"The devil with orders!" barked Dusty. "This is emergency! Put me through pronto!"

"Would if I could, captain, but it can't be done. His incoming call switch is down. I can't get through."

Dusty cursed.

"Then bang on his door!" he roared. "I don't give a damn what you do, but tell him I'll be there in ten minutes—and I've got to see him!"

The voice at the other end started to mumble more protests, but Dusty hung up on him and tore out through the door. Bolton was waiting with a car, but a red-faced tailor-made transport lieutenant was bellowing orders at him. Dusty leaped in behind the wheel, and shoved the lieutenant off the running-board, all in the same movement.

"Clear out!" he snapped. "The sergeant acted on my orders. I'll take all responsibility."

The lieutenant gulped, started to say something but leaped out of the way as Dusty slipped electro-mesh gears and the car shot forward. Thumb jammed down on the siren he sent the car thundering straight across the field and up onto the highway that lead straight into the heart of the capital.

He had said ten minutes, but he actually had three minutes to spare when he braked to a screaming stop in front of the Air Force building, located directly opposite the War Department Building. Slamming open the door he piled out and raced up the steps, with Bolton tagging his heels. Tearing into the first empty elevator he rapped the astonished operator on the arm.

"Sixty-first floor—snappy!" he barked.

DUSTY CHARGED
THE DOOR

Even as the last flew from his lips, the operator had slammed the doors shut and was shooting the car upward. At sixty-one Dusty rushed out and over to a staff major seated at a desk in the corridor.

"You told him I was coming?" he demanded.

The staff major stood up.

"I told you, Captain Ayres, that it was impossible to—here, where are you going? Come back, captain!"

But Dusty wasn't listening. With Bolton clinging to him like a shadow, he raced down the hall, through the end door, and down a corridor to a door upon which was printed:

General W.B. Bradley
Chief of Air Force Staff
PRIVATE

"Private, hell!" snorted Dusty, and tried the knob.

It was locked. From the inside, obviously. Bunching his right fist he pounded it against the wooden panel.

"General Bradley!" he shouted. "Open up, sir!"

The roar of his voice opened up half a dozen other doors, but not General Bradley's. In no time at all the corridor was filled with men and officers of all ranks. The staff major had panted up, and he grabbed Dusty by the arm.

"What the devil do you think you're doing, Captain Ayres?" he thundered. "Get away from that door, or—"

He didn't finish the rest. With a side sweep of his arm, Dusty sent him reeling back into the arms of an ordnance captain.

Then he smashed his fist against the door panel and shouted again. But the door didn't open.

For a split second Dusty scowled at it, and then, as that old familiar tingling sensation came to him, he stepped back a couple of paces and drew his service automatic. He leveled it at the outside lock.

"Stop it!" cried the staff major behind him. "Good God, are you out of your mind?"

Dusty's answer was to pull the trigger twice in rapid succession. The lock folded inward and the panel split wide open from top to bottom. Shoulders bunched, Dusty charged the door, and with a splintering crash it swung inward. Unable to check himself he went sprawling on his hands and knees. As he started to jerk up straight a sweet, sickish odor filled his nostrils. And instantly his head began to swim.

Realization and action were one. He spun around, slammed into Sergeant Bolton and virtually hurled him out into the corridor.

"Outside—stand back!" he choked. "The room's full of gas."

CHAPTER 4
"I AM POISONED!"

THE WARNING was really unnecessary. The sweet odor had already poured out into the corridor. Choking and gagging the crowd fell back like magic. All except Dusty and Bolton. Dusty even tried to shove him away but the non-com simply shook his head and crammed his handkerchief over the lower part of his face. He was actually starting into the room again when Dusty grabbed him.

"Get a medico—pronto!" Dusty barked.

Then bunching his own handkerchief over his face he charged into the room. His eyes smarted, and blurred everything. Inside the door he stopped long enough to catch up a chair, and holding his breath he swung it over his head and hurled it through a set of French windows on his left.

The instant it left his hands he ran over to a big desk on the far side of the room, and around in back of it. What he saw made him gasp involuntarily, and the fires of hell itself ate into his lungs. For one horrible second it was all he could do to fight off the swirling wave of nausea that swept over him. But he won and dropped down on one knee.

Sprawled out, and seemingly lifeless, behind the desk, their faces turned a terrible purple green, were General Bradley, and Jack Horner, known to a selected few as Agent 10!

Each man's hands were clutching his throat. And the neck of each tunic had been ripped apart. The eyes were closed, and the position of the bodies on the floor indicated that both had tried to reach the door but had collapsed from the sweet-smelling fumes before they had taken more than two steps.

His heart skipping a beat, Dusty leaned over and pressed his ear to each man's chest. Then he straightened up with an inward prayer of thankfulness. Life still flickered in both men. Handkerchief clenched between his teeth, Dusty caught General Bradley under the armpits and dragged his limp body over to the smashed window, through which fresh air now poured.

Going back he grabbed hold of Agent 10 and dragged him over. That done with, he staggered from window to window, and slammed them all open wide. But by the time he had opened the last, his head felt like a ball of fluff on his shoulders, and his feet seemed to be walking on fleecy clouds.

Unable to move another foot he let his body slump outward over the window sill. Hanging head downward, he sucked blessed fresh air into his lungs. His brain was roaring like storm waves thundering against a seawall, and the skin of his face became so taut that he half unconsciously expected it to split apart any second.

The next thing he knew, some one was pulling him up onto his feet, and forcing a bitter liquid between his teeth. He tried to spit it out, but something clamped over his nose and he had to swallow.

The reaction was instantaneous. Like the drawing aside of a curtain, things ceased to be blurred any longer, and he found himself staring into the grinning features of Sergeant Bolton. He managed a smile, and steadied himself on his feet.

"I'll be owing you money, before we're through," he grunted.

The non-com chuckled.

"I'm just getting the breaks, sir," he said. "Feel better now?"

Dusty nodded and glanced about the room. It was filled with wide-eyed officers gaping at him. But the bodies of General Bradley and Jack Horner had disappeared. He impulsively pointed his hand at the spot where he'd left them by the window.

"What—where—?" he stammered out.

"In the outer corridor, sir," Bolton explained. "The medico's working on them. He gave me this stuff for you."

The non-com held out a small vial half-filled with a brownish liquid. Dusty made a wry face, pushed it away and started toward the door. He took a couple of tottering steps before Bolton could grab him.

"Easy, sir, easy!" he cried. "You can't do anything now. You've done plenty already. Sit down, sir. The stuff's gone from the room."

Dusty shook his head.

"Feel swell," he mumbled. "I've got to see them. They can't die, see? They just can't die!"

"They won't, they won't!" pleaded Bolton, trying to hold him back. "The medico said you got them just in time. He's bringing them to, now."

BUT THE non-com might just as well have pleaded with Niagara Falls to run uphill for all the good it did stopping Dusty. Practically pulling Bolton along with him, he charged through the gaping mob and out through the door into the corridor. To his right and at the far end, white-jacketed men were working over two prostrate forms. With a groan Dusty lurched and stumbled down to them.

"How are they—how are they?" he gasped.

One of the white-jacketed men shoved him aside without bothering to look at him.

"Clear out! Didn't we tell you to keep back?"

Hardly realizing what he was doing Dusty grabbed the man and spun him around.

"Answer my question—will they live?"

The medico recognized him instantly, and checked the hot rush of words to his lips. He nodded and gently but firmly pulled Dusty's hand from his arm.

"Yes," he said. "Fortunately they didn't get too much of the stuff. Falling to the floor saved them, I guess. Now, just sit tight. They'll come around in a few minutes."

Fists clenched, face taut and grim, Dusty watched the medicos work on the two limp figures. And then, after a thousand years it seemed, Jack Horner's chest began to heave up and down. And a moment after that he opened blood shot eyes. The purple-green hue had disappeared from his skin and left it a chalky white. It was the same with the skin of General Bradley's face. And finally, he also opened his eyes.

At a signal from one of the medicos the others lifted up the two men and propped them, backs against the wall. Like stuffed dummies they sat there, slowly moving their heads, and blinking stupidly. It was more than Dusty's taut nerves could stand. He pushed through the ring of medicos and knelt down in front of Agent 10.

"Jack!" he cried. "Out of it, kid! It's Dusty!"

The Intelligence man's eyes, that had been gawking off to the left slowly swept back to meet his. For a moment they gaped blankly. Then, suddenly, their glassiness faded away, and the man's lips slid back in a crooked grin.

"You, eh?" he whispered hoarsely. "What the hell—I was having a swell dream about you. You were teaching me to loop—and was I lousy!"

Before Dusty could say anything, one of the medicos put a glass of brownish liquid to Jack Horner's lips.

"Drink this," he ordered firmly. "No—slowly."

Agent 10 drained it to the bottom, coughed violently, shook his head and screwed up his face.

"My God!" he gasped. "I've been poisoned!"

As though the words had suddenly released a hidden spring in his brain, he sat up straight and gazed wild-eyed around.

"What the hell?" he cried out. "What—where's General Bradley? That damn corporal—get that rat corporal!"

Still babbling he staggered to his feet. A medico grabbed him.

"Hold it!" he snapped. "You'll be O.K. in a minute."

Agent 10 nodded dully and leaned against the wall, just as General Bradley came back to his senses. Jack Horner's actions were but kindergarten stuff compared with the Chief of Air Force Staff.

The man roared and thundered about like a tornado gone berserk, and it took three medicos to pin him back against the wall. After they had held him there for a few seconds, he quieted down just as suddenly as he had roared up. And it was then that his eyes focused on Dusty. He pushed the medicos to one side.

"Ayres!" he cried. "How long have you been here?"

"You can thank him, sir, for being alive," spoke up one of the medicos. "He broke down your office door in time. As a matter of fact, just in time. How do you feel, sir?"

Bradley frowned at him a moment, as though unable to understand the question. Then—

"Eh? Oh, I feel fine. Make a report on this Thompson, and thanks. That's all. Ayres, come along with me. You too, of course, Horner."

As though nothing at all had happened the Chief of Air Force Staff waved them all aside and started down the corridor. Agent 10 followed, and so did Dusty. But as the pilot suddenly caught the look on Sergeant Bolton's face, he paused and motioned the man over. The non-com's face was all eagerness as he practically leaped the distance between them.

"Stick around, sergeant," Dusty told him in a low voice. "Maybe there'll be another job for you, and maybe there won't. But stick around, anyway."

"Horses won't move me, sir," grinned the other.

Dusty nodded and ran after Bradley and Horner. As the Chief of Air Force Staff reached the door of his office, he stopped short and stared at it wide eyed.

"Huh!" he grunted. "Guess we'd better use Stafford's."

GOING DOWN the corridor to the third door on the right he shoved it open and motioned Dusty and Jack Horner inside. Following them in, he locked the door on the inside, darted sharp eyes about the room, and went over and dropped into the chair behind the desk. And then, seemingly oblivious to their presence, he snapped up the switch of the inter-office phone on the desk, and yanked the receiver off the hook.

"Get me Major Jordon, Intelligence!" he barked into the transmitter.

51

And then a moment later.

"Jordon? Bradley speaking. A general alarm for a man known as Corporal Haggard, attached to the orderly department, Air Force building. About five feet-nine or ten. Dark skin and dark brown hair. Eyes brown, too. I want him caught, alive if possible. But, shoot if you have to. Eh, what's that?—the charge is murder. Yes, murder.

"He's a Black agent, of course. Now, never mind questions. Get busy on it at once. And keep in touch with me. Oh, wait a minute. Double your men in this building, and have them check up on every living soul here. Understand? Right. 'Bye!"

The general slapped the receiver back on the hook, placed both elbows on the edge of the desk and rubbed his face with both hands.

"I'll smell that damn stuff for weeks!" he rumbled. "Ugh!"

Removing his hands from his face, he looked directly at Dusty.

"So Horner and I owe you a vote of thanks, eh?" he grunted. "Well, we extend them, double, with pleasure!"

"Glad you came around O.K., sir," said Dusty quietly. "But, just what happened?"

Bradley and Horner exchanged glances.

"Did you note the time, by any chance, Horner?" asked the Chief of Air Force Staff.

Agent 10 scowled thoughtfully.

"Not exactly, sir," he said. "But, I'd say it was around eleven-thirty."

The other glanced at his watch and sat bolt upright.

"My God! It's after four now!"

"But, what happened, sir?" Dusty persisted evenly.

"A rat gassed us!" was the blunt reply. "We were sitting here talking when that damn orderly corporal came in. He gave it to us both in the face with a gas gun, and—well that's the last I remember. How about you, Horner."

"The same, sir," nodded Agent 10. "Yet, I have a hazy recollection of seeing him put something over his face—a gas mask, probably."

Dusty's heart was pounding against his ribs, and the blood was racing through his veins. He leaned toward Agent 10.

"Eleven-thirty, Jack? You're sure of that time?"

"Practically," nodded the other. "Maybe five minutes either way. Why? Has anything happened?"

Dusty ignored the question. His eyes flew to General Bradley's face.

"There's a short-wave broadcasting set in your office, isn't there, sir?" he asked quickly. "I think I saw one."

"Correct," said the other. "I use it for personal orders when I don't want to waste time going over to the main station on the War Department building. But, what about it?"

"Plenty, I think, sir," said Dusty grimly.

And then in crisp and right to the point sentences, he told them of all that had happened since he left the drome of High Speed Group 7. The other two listened to the very end in stunned silence.

"Just what the true hook-up is," finished Dusty in a whirlwind of words, "I don't get, for the life of me. Tell me, general, what orders did you really send out?"

The senior officer appeared to have difficulty finding his tongue. He was like a man in a trance—a trance of fear, or indescribable horror.

"Just one," he finally got out. "The one grounding you. The Twentieth bombers—oh God. Damn their souls! Damn their rotten souls to hell! By God, I'm going to see General Horner myself, and—"

He stopped short, glanced at young Horner.

"I'm sorry, son," he said softly. "For the moment I forgot."

Agent 10's lips went back in a forced smile.

"Quite all right sir," he said. Then turning to Dusty, "You didn't see what got the bombers?" he asked. "Didn't see any other plane—a Black Invader ship, I mean?"

"Nothing but the flash of light, and the skyful of shooting stars immediately afterward," answered Dusty. "Obviously, whatever it was didn't get them all that time. That garbled radio message I picked up is proof that some of them got through."

"Through to where?" Bradley suddenly bellowed savagely. "That's the point—just the point! A perfect secret bombing raid has been wiped out before it even got started."

"But, sir," Dusty put in, "it's possible that the few that did get through, did some damage."

"You don't understand, Ayres," said the other. "Twentieth bombers were standing by for orders to smash the Canadian seaports held by the Blacks. They didn't even know themselves what their objective was to be. Only I knew it. And I never sent the order to them!"

"I think I get it now," said Dusty. "The crazy course they took, I mean. The Hawk wanted to be sure to kill a bunch with one stone—the bombers and myself. In order to be sure and nail my train he had to fake orders, after Twenty was in the air, for them to swing east over Springfield."

"Probably," nodded Bradley. "However, we'll never know— that is, if they all went down. But, you spoke of the Hawk, Ayres. Why the Hawk? What makes you think he's behind it?"

Dusty's smile was tight.

"The style in which it was attempted," he said. "Any other Black who wanted me out of the way would just try to sneak up on me and bury some steel in my back. But not the Hawk. His way would have to be fancy, spectacular. Right, Jack?"

"I think you are, Dusty," Agent 10 nodded. "Ten to one he was back of the job, and back of that anonymously written newspaper flier, too. You've seen one I suppose?"

"And how!" Dusty grated. Then to General Bradley, "Is that why you grounded me, sir? Because you thought I might go haywire?"

To his surprise the Chief of Air Force Staff shook his head.

"No. That is, not exactly. We were—I guess you better tell the story, Horner."

Agent 10 didn't start talking directly. Instead, he half turned and stared out the window, his still rather pale face set in grim lines. Then presently he turned to Dusty.

"It begins a few months back," he said quietly. "Remember

that death-beam ship the Blacks swiped, and then we grabbed back from them?"

Dusty grinned.

"I don't think I'll ever forget it," he said.

"WELL," CONTINUED young Horner, "there was one major fault with the beam unit. It was only good for a certain length of time—as you probably remember. Anyway it was returned to the Bureau of Scientific War Research for Professor Colgan—the murdered Schrouder's assistant, you know—to get to work on. Colgan was to try and develop some way for the disintegrator beam unit to be regenerated while the plane was in flight.

"Well, Colgan failed to do that—but his failure resulted in an even greater success. He discovered a means of trapping and controlling C.R.D."

"C.R.D.?" grunted Dusty at his pal paused for breath. "And what in the world might that be? Sounds like a radio call signal to me."

"C.R.D. destroyed those bombers, and very nearly resulted in your death," young Horner said quietly. "The initials stand for Cosmic Ray D. As you know, science has found out that this power formerly referred to as simply the cosmic ray, is really made up of several elements.

"Three of these have been discovered and segregated. In other words, C.R. A, B and C. But it was Professor Colgan who segregated C.R.D. Don't ask me to explain it technically. I'm not a scientist. I only know that it is something like ribbon lightning, or chain lightning if you wish. And its force is about one hundred thousand times greater than the lightning that splits the front yard apple tree in a thunder storm. Colgan could explain it in detail—if he were alive."

Dusty sat up straight.

"Good God," he cried, "don't tell me that they got him like they got Schrouder who figured out the disintegrator beam?"

Agent 10 shook his head.

"No," he said evenly. "He was killed by us."

For a moment Dusty's tongue refused to move. He stared hard at his pal of a hundred-and-one wild and dangerous adventures of war.

"You—you mean—?" he got out, and stopped.

Young Horner nodded solemnly. "The day before yesterday," he said. "Yeah, I can hardly believe it myself. Colgan has been with the Bureau of Research for four years. Think of it, over three years before the Blacks declared war on us."

Dusty groaned out a curse.

"And we risked our necks to get that beam unit, only to turn it over to him!" he grated. "But, hell—it doesn't make sense. You say he developed, or segregated this C.R.D.? Well, why didn't he turn it over to the Blacks? Why isn't he up with them?"

"That's obvious, Ayres," spoke up General Bradley. "Don't you see, it doubled his usefulness to the enemy to be working right in our Research Bureau. Not only was he able to develop formulas, and so forth, that he could turn over to his own side later, but at the same time he was able to keep track of every new scientific war development that we made."

BEFORE THE OTHER INTELLIGENCE MEN COULD REACH THE PLANE, IT TOOK OFF

"Yeah, that's true, of course," Dusty grunted. Then to young Horner, "What about the shooting?"

"The details of that, I also got second hand," said Agent 10.

"Intelligence was beginning to suspect Colgan, as he was known in this country. Anyway, a watch was put on him.

"It was discovered that every night he took a walk to a field a few miles south of Alexandria.

"He just walked there and back. But the night before last he carried a package—a rather large and heavy package. He also carried a flashlight. He went to the middle of the field, and signaled with the flash light. A plane landed, a Black Invader ship. Colgan ran over to it, and our men trailing him closed in. One of them actually jumped into the cabin, and shot Colgan. Colgan fell out and onto the ground. And before the other Intelligence men could reach the plane it took off and disappeared—with the package."

"And, I suppose that package—?" began Dusty.

"Contained everything relative to Colgan's work on C.R.D." Agent 10 finished for him. "Notes, formulas—everything. He'd stripped his laboratory bare. As a matter of fact, I think that he planned to make his escape in the plane."

"And the plane wasn't sighted again?" asked Dusty. "Didn't you send out an S.O.S. or anything?"

"We did everything, Ayres," General Bradley spoke up again. "And we failed. No, everything except one item. The Intelligence man who was flown away in the plane, got one message back to us. Here, read it yourself. It came through this morning, through certain channels that need not be mentioned."

The Chief of Air Force Staff pulled a crumpled sheet of paper from the inside pocket of his tunic, and handed it to Dusty.

The pilot smoothed it out and glanced at the hastily scrawled words.

10—Refuse all demands by Blacks. Will find a way out myself—X 34.

Dusty sucked in his breath sharply as he read the signature. His eyes flew to Agent 10's face.

"Good God!" he cried. "X Thirty-four! Why that's your—"

He stopped short at the look on the Intelligence man's face. Young Horner was battling desperately to keep jangled nerves under control.

"Yes," he murmured thickly. "General Horner, my father, was the man who got Colgan, and was flown away in the plane!"

CHAPTER 5
RAT BAIT

AS AGENT 10 stopped talking a heavy, charged silence settled over the room. Dusty inwardly cursed himself for the inability to say something. Yet, the words—adequate words, would not come to his lips. He simply sat like a man of stone, his eyes locked with those of young Horner's. And then hardly realizing it, he put out his hand gripped the other's arm and squeezed hard.

"We'll get him back, kid," he said grimly. "Don't worry, we'll get him back."

The Intelligence man managed a stiff smile.

"Thanks," he said. "I knew that would come from you. The

Blacks have tried to bargain with me already. This came through by code radio about an hour after my father's message arrived."

Stuffing a hand in his pocket he pulled out a short length of radio message type. Dusty took it, and glanced at more printed words.

> To Chief of General Staff, Washington, D.C.
>
> General Horner of your Intelligence Department is now our prisoner. He has been unharmed and will be exchanged for the body of his son, known as Agent 10.
>
> (signed) The Black Hawk.

Dusty's eyes were agate as he looked up from the message. "The rat!" he grated. "The dirty low down rat! Playing the same old trick again, eh?"

"And it won't get him a thing!" said young Horner grimly.

"Right!" nodded Dusty. Then as an after thought, "You mean—?"

"That we're not gambling for individual lives," answered the Intelligence man. "This war is a matter of life or death for an entire country. My father hammered that into me long ago."

Dusty said nothing but the look of frank admiration that he gave Jack Horner, said plenty. Though his father was in the hands of the enemy, and young Horner could buy his freedom with his own life, he was refusing to do so. Refusing, not to protect his own skin, but because the true issue at stake was the fate of a nation—and in light of that, personal items had no part at all.

"We'll get him back, kid," Dusty repeated with savage conviction. "But, let's check over a few things first. You must have had some kind of a plan. I still don't get that grounding order."

The last was directed at General Bradley, but it was Horner who answered.

"That was my idea," he said quietly. "The Blacks getting the C.R.D. stuff, and that newspaper flier coming out, all at the same time, worried me a bit."

"Worried you?" frowned Dusty.

"In a way, yes," the other nodded. "I was afraid that the Hawk would send you another of his challenges—and that you'd go after him hell-bent."

Dusty's lips went back in a tight grin.

"I probably would have," he said.

"Exactly," nodded Agent 10 solemnly. "And not knowing what you were running up against, it would have been just too bad for you. So I induced General Bradley to ground you until I could get in touch with you and put all the cards on the table. You see, I was planning to go up to your field this afternoon. Well—you know why I was delayed."

"Yeah," grunted Dusty. "But about that newspaper flier. I suppose the idea was to get my goat and send me haywire—which it darn near did. But, has it been traced down? I mean, do you know where it was printed?"

"In a general way, yes," spoke up Bradley. "Our experts tell us that the type is of a Canadian font, so they were probably printed by the Blacks and distributed through their agents in this country."

"What a dumb stunt!" muttered Dusty. And then inwardly

took back his words as he realized how very close it had come to working out, just as it was planned.

For a moment no one spoke. Each seemed to be busy with his own thoughts. Dusty glanced at the other two, expecting them to say more. And when they didn't, he put the question that was uppermost in his mind.

"Well, so what? What's our next move?"

Bradley scowled and Agent 10 gestured helplessly. And it was he who answered.

"I don't know, Dusty," he said bitterly. "Damned if I know! That's one reason, the main one, why I wanted to have a talk with you. I had hoped that we might work out some way to recover the C.R.D. stuff before the Blacks could do anything about it, but after what's happened today, that idea is sunk.

"That devil, Colgan, played his part perfectly. He must have got news of his discovery through to the Blacks. Hell, that's obvious. They had a plane all built for the unit—built and waiting for Colgan. They didn't get him, but they got the formula and secret papers, which is the important thing."

THE INTELLIGENCE man allowed his voice to trail off into silence. Never before, in all of their wild, death-defying adventures, had he ever seen his secret-service pal so utterly depressed. Impulsively he reached out and rapped a clenched fist against the man's shoulder.

"Snap it up!" he barked. "We've cracked tougher ones than this before. We'll just buzz up and take the damn thing away from them—just like we took the beam ship away!"

"I admire your fighting spirit and determination, Ayres," put in General Bradley quietly. "But, I'm afraid you overlook one very important fact—just where would you go? So far, we have no idea where their operating base is located. We had been counting on our Intelligence men working behind their lines to get some sort of word through to us. But—even they have failed. And—well, each passing hour makes the situation more desperate than before. If they are able to produce the thing on a large scale—"

He left the rest unfinished, and simply implied the rest with a movement of his hands. Dusty leaned toward him.

"I suggest that we make them show us where it is, sir," he said.

The Chief of Air Force Staff gave him a blank look.

"Eh? What's that you say?"

"Let's make them show us where it is," Dusty repeated. "Now, let's check-back again. I'd say that the Hawk is pretty keen to get my scalp. Being cuckoo in a lot of ways, he probably figured that that flier stuff would get my dander up, and that I'd come gunning for him. Or as Horner, here, just said, he'd send me some kind of a challenge and then wipe me out with this C.R.D. thing of Colgan's.

"Well, Jack checked that when he had you ground me. So, that left it for the Hawk to get me some other way—hence, those dizzy orders to come down here by train. Now, in the meantime there was the secret bombing squadron to knock off. So the Hawk had to postpone my finish—hence the delay message sent to Colonel Parks at the Springfield station. Or maybe, making up the train was the cause for that delay.

"Anyway, I don't think that everything went off as they planned. At least I'm still alive. Now, maybe they know it, and maybe they don't—so, let's make sure that they do know it."

General Bradley shrugged.

"And what good would that do us?" he grunted. "Dammit, if we could only catch that rascal orderly corporal we might get something out of him! If your assumptions are correct, Ayres, that man was almost in constant contact with the Hawk—and on my private radio, too. I—"

The senior officer left the rest hanging in mid-air, as at that instant there came two crashing revolver shots beyond the locked door. They had not even died to the echo before Dusty was out of his chair and bounding across the room. Pulling his service automatic free with one hand, he unlocked the door and jerked it open with the other.

On the floor just outside lay the crumpled figure of a signal corps private. He was face down, one arm and a leg crumpled under him, and in the outflung other hand was a blunt-nosed automatic. A dozen yards down the hallway, face deathly white, and a gun clutched in his hand stood Staff Sergeant Bolton.

"My God, what's this all about?"

Dusty ignored General Bradley's startled cry behind him. Holstering his gun, he walked up to Bolton.

"What happened, sergeant?" he asked quietly.

The sound of his voice seemed to drag the non-com out of a paralytic trance. His stiff body relaxed, and some of the color came back into his face. He stared down at his gun then over at the dead man near the door.

"I was waiting as you ordered, sir," he began in a flat voice. "Waiting over here in this el in the wall."

He paused long enough to turn and point where he had been standing. And then, "I saw him sort of easing down the corridor. Guess he didn't see me. He went up to that door and put his ear against it. Then he took something out of his pocket—looked like a rubber tube with a bulb on it, to me—and started to push it into the keyhole. I yelled at him then and he just spun toward me and swung up his gun and—well, I beat him to the draw—his aim was pretty bad."

As the non-com spoke the last his eyes traveled to a spot on the wall to his right. Dusty followed the look and saw where a bullet had buried itself in the plaster.

BY THEN an excited crowd had gathered in the corridor, and everyone was asking everyone else all sorts of unanswerable questions. Deaf to those fired his way, Dusty motioned to Bolton to follow and went back to where General Bradley and Jack Horner were bending over the dead man. The Chief of Air Force Staff was gingerly fingering a foot of thin tubing, to one end of which was fitted an oval bulb. Dusty already knew what it was.

"Careful, sir!" he said squatting down. "I think there is some gas in that bulb that was meant for us. Sergeant Bolton, here, stopped him just in time."

Bradley shot a sharp glance at the non-com and demanded to know just what had happened. The answer was exactly what Dusty had been told, only Bradley didn't seemed so pleased.

"Too bad you had to kill him," he grunted. "It would have helped to find out who he was."

"Don't worry about that, sir," spoke up Jack Horner, who had turned the dead-man over. "Look here, sir."

As he spoke he reached down and peeled off fake shaggy eyebrows. Then he took a strip of putty off the bridge of the nose, and two rubber plates from out of the mouth that gave a deceptive fullness to the originally sunken cheeks.

"Good God!" gasped Bradley, as he stared at the man anew. "Why—that's that damn orderly corporal!"

"Exactly, sir," young Horner concurred. "And I think that Sergeant Bolton is to be congratulated on preventing him from making good the second time."

Eyes a trifle wider, General Bradley slowly straightened up. He stared at the non-com a moment and then gave a little jerking nod of his head.

"Yes, yes, of course," he said. "I'll see that you're mentioned about this, sergeant. But, why have you been waiting around here?"

Dusty answered for Bolton, and then added, "With your permission, sir, I'd like to have Sergeant Bolton join our little meeting."

Before Bradley could do, or even say, anything, Dusty pushed the non-com into the room and motioned him to a chair. The senior officer started to speak, then changed his mind, and instead, gave orders for the dead body to be cleared away. And then with Jack Horner at his heels he came back into the room and shut the door. The eyes he fixed on Dusty were not particularly pleasant.

"I'm sure we all owe Sergeant Bolton a lot, Ayres," he got out gruffly. "But, this other matter is one of—"

"I know, sir," Dusty interrupted. "But Sergeant Bolton fits very nicely into a plan that has come to me. A plan, whereby we may be able to get out of the difficulty we've landed in."

The other was still skeptical, and the expression on his face showed it. He glanced at Jack Horner. The Intelligence man nodded.

"I'll back Captain Ayres in anything, sir," he said. "His vouching for Sergeant Bolton is good enough for me."

Bradley coughed a bit.

"Very well," he mumbled. "Now, what is this plan, Ayres?"

"A few minutes ago, sir," Dusty began, "you asked me what good it would do us to let the Blacks know that I'm still alive. Well, I think it would do this much—it would at least bring the Hawk out into the open again. Somehow, I've got the hunch that he feels as I do—that our next meeting is going to be the last for one of us. One of us is going to step out of the picture. So, I suggest that we work it from the original angle—the angle that the Hawk was counting on to work."

As Dusty paused for breath, General Bradley frowned and moved restlessly in his chair.

"Get to the point, Ayres!" he growled. "What do you mean by all that?"

Dusty cursed inwardly.

"Simply this, sir," he said. "Let me play up to the Hawk. I'll play up to him as though I were throwing down the gauntlet, because of that newspaper flier. I'll challenge him to an air scrap—a scrap to the finish—over the New Hampshire-Canada line at, say, seven dawn tomorrow. And—"

"But good heavens, man!" Bradley burst in. "If he meets you with that confounded thing, you won't stand a chance!"

"If he meets me, yes sir," Dusty replied evenly. "But, you see, I won't be there. Between now and that time, I'm going to hunt out where he keeps that C.R.D. job. And when I do—well, I'll wait until I do."

Jack Horner, who had been listening eagerly, groaned aloud as Dusty paused.

"What the devil, Dusty?" he grunted. "That doesn't get us any place! How in hell do you expect to find it between now and dawn? Particularly, when none of us has the faintest idea where it might be!"

"None of us?" echoed Dusty. "I've got a pretty good hunch where it might me. And just as soon as it's dark, Bolton is going to fly me up there and let me off."

"And that hunch?" asked Horner.

"C Fifty-six!" Dusty shot right back at him. "The area where B Flight of the Twentieth Bombers was trapped. Why was B Flight allowed to go way the hell up in that God-forsaken area? Why?—so that the Hawk could show his gang how it was done. That's my guess. And I doubt that they were allowed to go up there—I think that they were either forced, or lured. Anyway, I'm going to put my chips on C Fifty-six!"

Agent 10's brows came together in a thoughtful frown.

"I wonder if you've hit the nail on the head?" he murmured, more to himself. Then in louder tones, "But why all this scrap at dawn stuff? And why not you and I go up there?"

Dusty shook his head.

"NIX," HE said. "Just in case some more rats, like that one Bolton popped, are hanging around, I want to make it look like the real thing. For you and me to be seen taking off, would sink the idea right at the start. As for Bolton, he could be flying me back to my field—back to get the Silver Flash tuned up, and so forth.

"The main idea for the challenge for a scrap at dawn, is just this! We don't know what that devil may do next, and we've got to keep his damn C.R.D. job out of the air as long as possible. My challenging him will do it, I think. He'll use up the time between now and dawn to make doubly sure that his ship, and his plans, for what he believes will be a swell show-down, are all set. See what I mean?"

As Agent 10 nodded but said nothing, Dusty turned to General Horner.

"I have your permission to carry it out, of course, sir?" he said in a matter-of-fact tone.

The senior officer regarded him shrewdly.

"An absolutely insane plan, if I ever heard one!" he snapped. And then with a shrug, "But, perhaps it will take an insane man to get us out of this mess. God knows we've got to do something, and damn soon, too!"

"Thank you, sir," grinned Dusty. "I'll sure try my best to be just that man. All right, Bolton, go down to the military field and make arrangements for a plane to fly me back to my drome tonight. I'll phone that you're coming. And be set by eight, sharp."

The non-com had considerable difficulty keeping the excitement out of his voice. To play any part in the plans of Dusty Ayres, was the greatest kick of his life thus far.

"Yes, sir!" he gulped, jumping up and making for the door. "Ready at eight sharp, sir."

"Seems like a good man, and I guess he's proved his stuff to you," grunted Agent 10, as the door closed on the non-com. "But, maybe Curly Brooks could handle that part of the job a bit better."

Dusty nodded.

"Undoubtedly!" he said. "But Bolton will go right back when I order him to. Maybe Curly wouldn't. And this has got to be a solo job this time. I've got to get the Hawk to thinking that I'm boiling over, and out to get him—all by myself."

"And God, but I hope you do, Dusty!" grated young Horner. "No—no I don't. I hope that pleasure will fall in my lap!"

Though the Intelligence man had not said it, Dusty knew that the thought of his father was uppermost in his mind. And two minutes later, when he left young Horner and Bradley, to go over to the main broadcasting station and hurl his challenge to the Black Hawk out over the air, he grimly told himself that not one but two jobs lay ahead of him—and that he would hand in his own chips rather than fail in either.

CHAPTER 6
THE INVISIBLE KILLER

A T EXACTLY five minutes of eight that evening, Dusty swung the staff car onto the tarmac of the Washington military field and braked to a gentle stop. Climbing out, he caught up a suitcase on the back seat, and walked rapidly over to where a small biplane cabin job rested, with prop slowly ticking over. Near the cabin door stood Bolton, smoking a last-minute cigarette with a couple of the field mechanics. As Dusty approached the three of them toed out their cigarettes, and saluted.

The pilot nodded and handed the suitcase to Bolton.

"Stow that inside, sergeant," he said. "But be careful! If you break those six bottles, my life won't be worth a dime at the field."

Bolton grinned, and handled the bag as though it were full of Tetalyne.

A few minutes later, with Dusty lounging back in the passenger seat, Bolton taxied out onto the runway, waited a moment for the flash from the signal tower, and then sent the plane racing down the floodlighted strip of concrete. As he swung up clear, and the floodlights blinked out, Dusty leaned forward and tapped him on the shoulder.

"Head north for ten minutes or so, Sergeant, at average altitude," he ordered. "Then circle her up to twenty-five thousand."

"Right, sir," said the non-com without turning his head.

Reaching back of his seat, Dusty pulled out the suitcase and opened it up. Instead of six bottles, it contained the complete uniform of a pilot of the Black Invader Air Service. Everything, from black skull-cap to highly polished half-length and black boots.

Stripping off his own uniform Dusty wiggled into the other. The fit was perfect, just as he had made sure that it would be. Reaching into the suitcase again he pulled out a small bottle of skin stain. Pouring some in the palm of his left hand, he "washed" his hands, and smeared the rest over his face, ears and neck. The result was a neat copperish glint to his otherwise more or less ruddy complexion.

"Jack sure knows his onions on makeup!" he grunted into the small pocket mirror he held up before him.

"Eh, sir?" echoed Bolton, and he started to turn his head.

He got it halfway around. His jaw dropped and his body froze stiff. Pop-eyed, he stared at Dusty, his lips moving but no sound coming from them. Finally his tongue virtually shoved the words out.

"My God! What the hell, sir? I—I thought you said there were bottles—"

"For the benefit of those two lads with you, Bolton," Dusty cut him off. "Can't take chances, you—hold it there! You're in a dive!"

Which was quite true. Not fully recovered from the shock, the non-com had unconsciously rammed the stick forward, and the plane was racing down through the night-darkened skies. He tore his eyes from Dusty long enough to ease the ship out of its dive and send it roaring heavenward again. Then he turned once more.

"Count on me to follow orders, sir," he stammered out. "But—well, I'd sure like to know what it's all about. I didn't gather much, when you were talking with General Bradley and Lieutenant Horner."

Dusty shrugged.

"Maybe when it's all over, Bolton," he said. "But, your main job is to get this ship back after I leave you at C Fifty-six. Incidentally, I'll take over, now."

The non-com failed utterly to conceal his disappointment as he changed seats with Dusty. But to his credit, he at least didn't put it in words.

The instant the stick was in his hand, Dusty forgot all about Bolton and concentrated on the job at hand. The ship was between fifteen and twenty thousand feet, headed dead-on for the drome of High Speed Group 7, and at the moment about fifty miles due west of New York City. All that checked up, Dusty snapped off the bug-light in the cabin ceiling and left only the instrument board cowl lamp glowing. And then as the ship went tearing forward through the night skies he gradually changed the course toward the northwest, and a point on Lake Ontario about halfway between Niagara Falls and Rochester, New York.

Swinging on robot control, he relaxed his grip on the stick, hunched forward, and stared thoughtfully out into the limitless void of black air.

STEP BY step he mentally reviewed everything that had

taken place since early morning. Some of the gaps in the sequence of cockeyed events he could fill in with sane reasoning. Others he could fill in with wild guesses. And still more he failed utterly to fill in, no matter how far he stretched his imagination.

The sum total of the whole thing was a very definite belief that a final and permanent show-down between himself and the Black Hawk was in the offing. A war between nations was marking time until two individuals had settled their scores against each other, once and for all.

Why he felt that way, he could not even satisfactorily explain to himself. This was not the first time, by any manner of means, that he had gone charging north to lock props and guns with the ace of the Black vultures. Yet, way down deep inside him, he knew absolutely that this time would be the last. When it was all over, either Dusty Ayres or the real Black Hawk would be dead for all eternity.

Unconsciously he clenched both fists and crushed them together.

Dusty was in the midst of these musings when steel fingers gripped hold of his shoulder and Sergeant Bolton's tensed voice crackled in his ears.

"Skipper!" he snapped, using the title for the first time. "I think a ship is tagging us!"

In one continuous movement, Dusty snapped off the cowl lamp, cut out robot control, and spun around in the seat.

"What's that?" he demanded. "You're sure?"

"Not positively!" came the other voice in the darkness. "But, back of us a bit and a thousand feet, or so, up!"

Throttling just a bit, to kill all traces of possible exhaust flame, Dusty swung the plane around and up to the right. Moving stick and rudder automatically, he pressed his face against the side cabin window and peered out into the enshrouding blanket of darkness.

Above him a few stars blinked and shimmered, and in the first moment of tensed excitement he mistook them for exhaust flares. But, almost immediately he realized what they were, and lowered his gaze toward the southern horizon. Five minutes later he swung the ship back onto its original course.

"Guess you must have been seeing things, Bolton," he grunted. "I don't think—"

He left the rest unsaid. At that moment the red signal light on the radio panel blinked rapidly. Shooting out his free hand he snapped on contact, and spun the wave-length dial. And then jerked up straight in the seat. Out of the cabin speaker unit came the shrill sing-songy sounds of the Black Invader high speed dot-dash code.

He listened to it for a few seconds, then risked the instrument board cowl lamp long enough to glance at the station directional finder dial. What he discovered made him suck in his breath in a sharp gasp.

The transmitter, sending out the signals, was located southeast of his position, and undoubtedly in the air. In fact, the directional needle quivered close to the reading of his own position, which meant that the transmitter was practically at the same latitudinal and longitudinal position as was his own ship.

As that truth came home to him, the high speed signals suddenly clicked off into silence, and the red signal light winked out.

"You must be right, Bolton!" he barked. "Here, take the left side. I'll take the right. Let me know the instant you see anything. And hang on—I may have to toss her about a bit."

Movement of Bolton over to the left cabin window was proof that the non-com had heard and was obeying orders. Jamming his face once more against the window on the right, Dusty peered savagely out into the darkness.

A flush of boiling rage burned up his neck and cheeks. And inwardly he cursed his luck. Unless he was crazy as a coot, his little plan was being nipped in the bud. Not knowing the Blacks' secret high speed code he hadn't been able to make anything out of the signals. But, he had the feeling that that wasn't necessary. The directional finder needle had told him enough. In short, it had told him that a Black ship was tagging his flight, and signaling progress—probably—to some other station.

For a moment he regretted the fact that he had not brought Agent 10 along. Perhaps Jack Horner could have made something out of the signals—at least confirmed or denied the fears that gripped him now.

YET, AS he strained his eyes out into the darkness, the most puzzling thought of all raced around inside of his head. Assuming that a mysterious Black ship was tagging him—how the hell was it doing it? For over half an hour, now, he'd been

THE WHITE DEATH

flying blind, all lights out. And there wasn't a single spark coming out of his exhaust stacks. The best piloting eyes in the world couldn't tag a lights-out ship on a night as dark as this. Hell, no, it couldn't possibly—

He killed the thought as a new one came to him.

"No!" he blurted out aloud. "Not unless he knows, or has a hunch, just where I'm headed! Hells bells!"

As the last rushed off his lips, the bottom seemed to drop out of everything. A sudden savage desire to wash out his original plan, and turn back, swept through him. The hell with this hit-and-miss, tag-in-the-dark stuff!

He'd go back and get the Silver Flash, and meet the Hawk over the New Hampshire-Canada line at dawn. Let the rat bring his mystery ship if he wanted to. He'd spotted the bum the advantage before. Right! And he'd do it again, and win.

And then, the savage yammer of aerial machine gun fire blasted his crazy jumble of thoughts into oblivion.

To his left, and from a few hundred feet above, twin streams of jetting flame ripped down toward him. For an instant he was caught ham-handed, and fingers of steel beat a savage tattoo against the outside wall of the cabin. And then with a roaring curse, he snapped himself out of the dumbfounded trance, and hurled the ship around and up on wingtip.

"The floor gun, Bolton!" he thundered. "Let drive at the flame!"

He did not turn his head, as he shouted the order. He kept his eyes glued on the spot in the dark sky that marked the source of those twin streams of jetting flame. And a moment later, as he jabbed his own trigger trips forward, he saw his target for the first time.

It was nothing but a rushing blur, faintly silhouetted against a background of night. But it was all that he needed. Once seen, he'd keep his eye on it, so long as the plane stayed close.

And sticking close seemed to be the one idea of the unknown pilot. Down rushed the shadow, its forward end spitting fire that mingled with the twin streams of jetting flame from Dusty's guns. Oblivious to the shower of steel that hammered against the nose of his ship, the Yank held his plane in an engine-roaring climb, and pumped bullet for bullet right back at the diving shadow.

Down raced one sky chariot of death, and up thundered the other. Two metal-clad, steel-spitting wasps tearing toward each other and utter destruction. And then the unknown pilot "broke."

The shadow cut around in a sharp bank to the left. In the split second allowed, Dusty was able to make out the barrel-shaped fuselage, and the stubby biplane wings. And then he slapped his own ship up in a bank in the opposite direction.

"Left—in front of you, Bolton!" he roared. "Let her rip!"

The last was practically drowned out as the non-com blazed away with his floor gun. Holding the plane in a tight spiral, Dusty slammed the ship around in two complete turns, and then flattened out so quickly that Bolton went rolling up against the cabin wall. The non-com's curse echoed in Dusty's ears, but he paid not the slightest attention. It was a make-or-break maneuver for him.

A split second later a harsh laugh spilled off his lips. The crazy trick had worked.

The unknown pilot had been misled by the flaming bursts from Bolton's gun. He had figured that Dusty's plane was following him around, and now he was cutting in for what he thought was a broadside attack.

But it wasn't. And a split second later Dusty's twin Brownings proved it. They yammered out a hail of steel and raked the "barrel" biplane from prop to tail wheel. Frantically, the other pilot tried to check his maneuver and slam into a flash half-roll and dive clear. But Dusty simply tapped rudder and blasted away all over again.

"Go back and learn a few things!" he roared into the yammer of his guns. "Go back and—"

He didn't finish.

At that moment something came tearing down from above. That something was a third airplane. Its make or type, Dusty could not see. He only saw the twin streams of jetting flame leaping down across the air space. Twin streams of jetting flame that buried themselves in the fuselage of the barrel biplane. For no reason at all, Dusty ceased his own fire and sat gaping as the newcomer hell-hammered the barrel biplane.

As a matter of fact, it was all over in the space of not more than ten seconds. The Black pilot, concentrating on half rolling clear of Dusty's fire, unknowingly put himself in a perfect cold-meat position for the third pilot. And that third pilot took full advantage of the moment.

TEN SECONDS, no more. And then a great tongue of

flame belched out from the barrel biplane and filled the surrounding heavens with its crimson glow. For a fleeting moment Dusty caught the vision of a bullet-spattered fuselage, splintered glass cockpit cowling, stubby one-bay wings, and a pointed snout. And then it all became a raging ball of flame slithering downward.

So bright and dazzling were the flames, that as Dusty glanced around to sight the mysterious third ship, he was unable to see it at all. And in almost no time the red glow fused out and the darkness of night closed in again.

"What the hell, skipper? What the hell?"

Bolton's lips babbled the question into Dusty's ear. He didn't answer at first. Simply sat rigid, straining his eyes out into the darkness for a glimpse of the unknown third plane. Then with a muttered curse he relaxed back in his seat.

"Your guess is as good as mine, Bolton," he grunted. "What did you see?"

"Nothing but that biplane crate going down in flames," was the answer. "Boy, but that was pretty shooting!"

"Yeah!" murmured Dusty thickly. "But, I'm getting damn tired of being on the wrong side of the question fence!"

As he spoke he snapped on radio, spun the wave-length dial and put his lips to the transmitter tube.

"Thanks whoever you are!" he called out over the air-waves. "How about showing yourself?"

Hardly had he spoken the words than he regretted his sudden action. After all, he wasn't so sure whether he was calling to friend or foe. And besides that, the very fact that he was broadcasting, was giving his position away to all those who might care to find it out.

He was in the act of snapping off the set and doubling back on his course, when the red signal light blinked and the speaker unit made sound.

"Calling two-four-two! Calling two-four-two!"

Dusty almost jumped out of his seat. Two-four-two was a wave-length reading that he and Curly Brooks once arranged to use when they didn't want listeners-in to identify either of them! For a moment he didn't know whether to laugh or curse. Curly Brooks? Could that have been Curly? That—?

He cut off the question and bent over the transmitter tube.

"On two-four-two!" he barked. "Go ahead!"

"Go on yourself, sap!" same the startling words out of the speaker unit. "And snap off that cabin ceiling light! Do you want the whole damn world to know?"

Dusty gulped.

"Huh?" he got out. "What the hell do you mean, ceiling light?"

"Yes, ceiling light!" repeated the speaker unit in more brittle tones. "A blind man can pick you up from ten miles away!"

Completely dumbfounded, Dusty instinctively bent his head back and stared at the ceiling of the plane. Everything was as dark as the inside of his black skull-cap. He blinked stupidly, bent back over the transmitter tube.

"Listen—" he began.

"Save it!" the voice of Curly Brooks in the speaker unit cut him off. "I'll see you later at M-29!"

And before Dusty could think up any answer to that one, the red signal-light blinked out and the speaker unit went silent. Curly Brooks had gone off the air!

CHAPTER 7
MIDNIGHT HELL

FOR ALMOST a minute, Dusty sat like a man turned to stone. But, there was plenty of activity inside his head. A crazy-quilt of cockeyed questions and answers revolved before his mind's eye, like a circular slide of a magic lantern. And nothing whatsoever made sense. "What's he mean, M-29, skipper?"

"How the hell da I know?" Dusty barked. "I've been over my head for the last hour!"

"Sorry, Skipper," said Bolton in a low voice. "Don't mean to bother you like that. I'll shut up."

The non-com's tone snapped Dusty back to his senses.

"I'm the one who should be sorry, Bolton," he said. "Skip it, if you can. I went off half-cocked. But, I really don't know what he meant by M-29. That's a map position reading on the Maine-Canada line."

"Do you know who he was, skipper?" Bolton asked, as Dusty fell silent.

Dusty told him.

"Lieutenant Brooks, eh?" echoed the non-com. "I've heard plenty about him. A wonderful pilot, too. But, how do you suppose he got way up here, skipper?"

85

"I'm not sure," answered Dusty slowly. "But, I've got a hunch, why—which isn't important at the moment. Listen, sergeant, bend your ears back a minute."

In a series of rapid-fire sentences, Dusty outlined everything that had happened.

"That's the story, cockeyed as it may sound," he finished up. "Now, out of fairness to yourself, I'm giving you a chance to make your own decision. It looks as though the Blacks are wise to what I'm up to—wise to the fact that I'm heading for C-56. So, there's no telling what we may run into. You may be able to put me down with no trouble at all. But you, also, may run into all hell breaking loose.

"Now, I more or less roped you into this thing. Say the word and I'll put you down on the Rochester field. We're still south of it, on our side. And don't think that I'll think any the less of you for calling all bets off. If I'd expected the idea to turn into such a mess, I'd have left you cooling your heels in Washington in the first place."

Sergeant Bolton didn't even hesitate. He reached out in the darkness and gripped Dusty's shoulder again.

"Let me put it this way, skipper," he said in a voice that trembled slightly with eager emotion. "Those slugs I fired a few minutes ago, were the first ones I've let drive at a real enemy in this man's war. Blasted staff-courier work has kept me so far from the fighting that I've had to read about it in the newspapers. And—well, I'm asking you to let me see as much of the real thing as I can this time. Either way it turns out will be jake with me."

Dusty chuckled.

"Good lad, Bolton," he said. "Guess I read you right the minute I met you. O.K.! Make yourself at home. We're going through non-stop, this time."

Checking position and altitude, Dusty altered his course a shade and roared up to maximum altitude. For the next hour neither of them spoke. Each was content, to mull over his own thoughts.

Eventually, though, Dusty, who had been constantly checking position, hall turned in the seat.

"Close to there now, Bolton," he said. "I'm going to start sliding down, with a dead engine. Be ready, the instant I touch rubber, to take over control. I'll jump and run for it. Don't wait an instant, see? Take right off and high-ball back, just as fast as you can. Report to General Bradley personally, and let him know that I got down. Get it all?"

"Got it, skipper!" grunted the other. "Count on me to get word to the General."

"Then, here we go!" yelled Dusty.

AND WITH that he killed the fuel throttle and ignition switch, and slanted the ship down in a long, flat glide earthward. Though all about him was nothing but utter darkness, he knew exactly where he was. Constant plotting of compass course against wind speed and drift made that possible.

He was a good two hundred miles behind the Blacks' first line of defense on the northern shores of Lake Ontario, and within sixty odd miles of the C-56 area. But just where he would eventually sit down was something that time alone would tell.

In a general way he knew that C-56 area was a hilly and rugged triangular plot of landscape, but with possible landing fields few and far between. In the last couple of thousand feet he'd have to pick out one—and trust to luck, that he'd get in and that Bolton would get out.

Hunched rigid over the stick he allowed the plane to float lower and lower, and silently battled with a new rush of fears and doubts that cropped up to taunt him. Out of the air had come a cry for help—the cry of a doomed voice. That voice had said—"down at C-56!" At that instant had been born the hunch he was now following through to its unknown end. What—

He killed the rest, and gritted his teeth.

"If I'm wrong, that'll be my tough luck!" he got out in a low fierce whisper.

And then, as though the gods of war had been waiting for him to say just those very words, the heavens split apart and all hell slammed down on top of him.

So sudden and so furious came the blow that for an instant his brain registered the belief that the plane he was flying had blown up in front of his face. But, that was only a flash impression, and then he saw the circle of jetting streams of fire showering down.

Dully he realized that they came from the gun muzzles of a ring of diving planes. And in the same instant he became conscious of the fact that not one single stream of jetting fire was coming directly at him. In short, he was hemmed in on all four sides, yet not directly in the line of fire.

But, he didn't pause to figure that out. He simply slapped up the switch, rammed the throttle wide open, and shoved the ship down to the vertical. A body smashed against his back, and curses from Sergeant Bolton's lips rang in his ears.

"Hang on, Bolton!" he yelled. "Our only chance is *down!*"

But the next few split seconds proved that even that wasn't much of a chance. The night raiders above raced him down foot for foot, and still didn't direct their fire directly at him.

Cursing his luck, dumbness, the fates, and particularly the possibility that he had not cut his engine soon enough to throw off any ground detector units that might have picked up his engine, he savagely held the plane in its mad dive toward the carpet of darkness.

The altimeter needle went haywire and slid around the dial face as though it would never stop. The over-revving engine in the nose howled out a wild song of protest, and the plane itself quivered and trembled as though the next second would see it go ripping apart in small-pieces.

Dusty ignored the hundred-and-one signs of overstrain. But with the inexperienced Bolton it was quite different. His shouted words were faintly audible above the roar of the engine and the whine of the wings in the wind.

"God, skipper—the wings will go!"

"You just hang on!" Dusty thundered back at him. "Leave the wings to me!"

Shimmering tracers streaking past told him that he had

gained a few hundred feet on the surprise attackers. He grinned tightly in the darkness, then steeled himself as he saw the ground itself come sweeping up.

"Now, baby, be nice!" he breathed, and eased back a bit on the stick.

The nose "bucked" and then started to swing up. And in that instant he hauled the stick all the way back into his stomach. For one hellish second a horrible helpless feeling swept over him. He seemed to almost feel the wings sag under the terrific strain. It was now or never—would they let go, or would they stay on?

It was an infinitesimal part of time itself. Yet to Dusty, it seemed an eternity before the nose curved all the way up and the plane shot skyward like a rocket gone crazy. Up, up, up it streaked, straight for a pair of eyes winking spitting tongues of yellow-red. Still hugging the stick back, Dusty jabbed both trigger trips and sprayed hot steel at those two winking eyes. For perhaps a second or two they continued to wink and then they went out for good. No, not for good, exactly, for as Dusty tore up past the diving plane he saw it start to flatten out and spin around so that its killer pilot could open up in a broadside attack.

But, that killer pilot might just as well have tried to maneuver around for a broadside attack at the moon. And the same for three or four of his comrades. Both guns yammering out a steady clatter of death, the Yank ship wing-screamed up and around and into the clear. Below it jetting streams of flame winked out, and blurred shadows came arcing up. Dusty grinned and eased around toward the north.

"Find me again, you bums!" he grunted. "Just try and find me again."

FLYING AT three-quarters throttle to kill all traces of exhaust flame he sneaked farther and farther northward. His exact position he had lost during the scrap, and he did not dare risk any lights to check. But that really didn't matter.

The main thing was, that he'd shaken off a flock of night killers. Yet, though that brought him a sense of joyous relief, at the same time it puzzled and worried him more than a little. How the devil had those Blacks found him? And how in hell had they been able to "box" him in so neatly in a pitch-dark sky?

They couldn't have done it better in broad daylight. There must have been a dozen ships in that brood at least. A dozen pilots, each of whom had picked him out of a midnight sky just as simply as though he had been flying with cabin and wing running lights ablaze. Memory of Curly Brooks' crazy words rushed back to add to his bewilderment. And impulsively he glanced up toward the cabin ceiling. It was still dark as the bottom of a coal mine.

"Curly must have been nuts, or drunk!" he grunted aloud. "Snap off the ceiling light? Hell—"

He cut the rest off short as Bolton touched his shoulder.

"They're swinging up behind us, skipper, I think!" he breathed fiercely. "Just got a flash of exhaust flame a couple of seconds ago. Shall I feed 'em some more from the floor gun?"

"No, no, don't do that!" Dusty got out quickly. "That would give our position away. Just sit tight. I'm going to swing to the left and around them."

Easing slowly around to the left he squinted out the cabin window. For a moment he didn't see anything, then suddenly he caught sight of the faint flicker of exhaust flames. They were a good quarter of a mile behind him, and at least three thousand above. He chuckled, straightened out, and eased the throttle back to the one quarter mark. The plane was just barely holding flying speed. As a matter of fact it mushed gently earthward.

And then it happened!

The red signal light on the radio panel blinked and a harsh voice crackled out of the earphones.

"Attention American plane below! If Captain Ayres is aboard, you may land at once. If he is not, then prepare to be destroyed!"

Heart thumping against his ribs, Dusty scowled in the darkness. Now what? Those rats had spotted the ship again! How the devil were they able to do it? Was he up against a bunch of miracle men, or something? Instinctively he pulled the ship around in a tight bank and went sliding south. But he had traveled less than a mile, when the speaker unit crackled sound again.

"It is useless to try and escape. You are in our sight every second. Answer my question—is one Captain Ayres aboard that plane?"

Dusty felt Bolton's hand clutch him; heard the non-com's excited words.

"Who's that, skipper? Who's that calling us?"

Dusty shrugged and shook his head. He didn't know. At the first sound of the voice he had thought that the Hawk himself was on the air. But in a matter of seconds he knew that that was not so. There was something decidedly different in this voice. The usual harshness of Black Invader speech, to be sure, yet blended in with it was a sort of high-keyed nasal twang.

On impulse he bent over the transmitter tube, started to speak, but checked himself as the strange voice came to him again.

"Your silence is sufficient. You are on my wave-length, and you have heard my words. Land at once, Captain Ayres! Drop flares and select a landing spot. We will withhold our fire."

"What are you going to do, skipper? He knows that you're aboard!"

Dusty didn't answer. He glared straight ahead in the darkness and wracked his brains for the answer to the whole thing. He felt like a mouse caught in a trap, with the cat just outside the cage waiting to pounce upon him no matter which way he moved. In some way, God knew how, those devils above were following his every move as though they were actually attached to his top wings. And yet, dammit, why were they playing him this way? What did it matter to them whether he was aboard the plane or not? Why in hell didn't they smack down in their killer attack, and get it over with? Why—?

"Hell, am I dumb!" he burst out loud. "That rat, the Hawk, wants to make sure. Yeah, just like I want to make sure about him. Well, let him worry awhile, damn his soul!"

With a savage movement he grabbed up the transmitter tube again.

"Captain Ayres hasn't got time to waste on second-raters!" he snapped. "He's after bigger fish. But I'm a buddy of his, and if you want a lesson, come on down and get it!"

AS THE last whipped off his lips, he rammed the throttle wide open, shoved the ship down in a short dive, and then pulled it up in a screaming zoom. The result was the one thing upon which he banked his chances. And the result was in his favor.

Down out of the midnight skies came rushing shadows—no more than blurred streaks cutting down across a canopy of faintly flickering stars. But that was enough for Dusty. His crazy dive and zoom had caught the others off guard. And before they could check their wild dives he was right in among them, and spraying hot steel in all directions.

The confusion that followed his insane attack brought a wild laugh to his lips. Like so many trapped birds the Blacks were striving frantically to cut around so that they could fire their own guns without the danger of hitting each other. As a matter of fact two of them crashed head-on, and seconds later a great ball of red flame hurtled downward.

But the success that was Dusty's, was only momentary. He had counted upon being able to rush around in the darkness and slap steel at any blur that whipped across his nose, whereas the Blacks would be helpless to return the fire, not knowing which blur was the American ship.

For a moment, yes, it worked. And then, suddenly, Dusty's

94

blood ran cold as steel fingers started to beat a savage tattoo against the sides of the cabin. An instant later the left cabin window splintered off into oblivion, and he was positive that something white-hot fanned his cheek.

Shouting, cursing in the same breath, he started hurling the cabin job about the sky in sheer reckless abandon. But, dives, loops, half- and full-rolls, spins, and every other scrap maneuver were all but a waste of time and strength. Hot steel continued to pound relentlessly against the ship, no matter what he did, or tried to do.

True, a certain satisfaction was his. A long burst from his own guns found the vitals of a Black ship, and the night heavens were again lighted up with a crimson glow as a third vulture slithered down into oblivion. But that was short-lived indeed. As though fired by the Devil himself, the phantom attackers tightened their web of singing steel more and more.

From a long way off, so it seemed, Dusty heard Sergeant Bolton's voice cry out with pain. He yelled to the non-com but received no answer. To turn around and grope for the man was impossible. And to snap on the cabin lights was plain suicide. There was but one thing to do—stick to his own job and pray for the best.

But as it had been at the very start, so did it continue to be a losing fight.

He was simply hurtling through a limitless void, pitch-black one instant, and ablaze with myriads of dazzling colored lights the next. And shooting stars, too. There—off to his left! That big one—heading right for him. Bank to the left! Left stick and rudder, dammit! It was getting close. Now, zoom—zoom you fool! It's going to hit you—hit you—hit—

CHAPTER 8
THE PHOSPHOROUS DISC

FROM A thousand miles away came the faint rumble of breakers on the sandy shores. No, the sound wasn't that of breakers—there was a purring, throbbing undernote. Yeah, more like the rolling tones of tom-tom drums. Yet—

Dusty groaned and blinked stupidly into a sea of utter darkness. God, how his head hurt. Felt like the scalp had been lopped clean off. Where the hell was he? And what had happened?

Somehow he knew that he was stretched out flat. There was a pain in his side; something sharp was digging into his ribs. No, the pain was in his right elbow. Yeah, his arm was twisted under him and the weight of his body was stretching the elbow ligaments. But, why couldn't he see? His eyes were open. God—had he gone blind? Or was this the way it was when you were dead?

"Dead, hell! Get up, you sap! Get up off your arm!"

His own grating voice echoed back to him, and served to clear his fogged brain. The next thing he realized he had propped himself into a sitting position with his hands. He closed his eyes, shook his head, and opened his eyes again. Still nothing but darkness.

And then as the sense of feeling came back to him, he was dully conscious of the fact that something stiff and bristly was brushing against his face. He put out a hand in the darkness, groped about and grabbed hold of thorny branches. The sharp barbs pricked his fingers and the palm of his hand, but he hardly felt the pain.

It took him a good two minutes to realize that the thorny branches were suspended above—that they dangled down on top of him. Grasping a couple more, he pulled hard. A clod of dirt and a shower of small stones spilled down on top of his head. He groaned and covered his head with his hands. Fine dust got in his eyes and smarted the lids to fire heat.

Hugging his head he tried, desperately, to think back. But his aching brain refused to function. He let his body slouch back but groaned again as his head struck against something blunt and hard. Twisting around, he felt about with his hands and touched an oval shaped stone embedded in a wall of crumbling clay. Impulsively he looked up. High above him a handful of tiny stars winked, almost ominously.

With a sharp gasp he struggled to his feet, took two steps forward and was brought up sharp by a clay and stone wall. Feeling his way with his hands, he followed the wall. It seemed to curve, and presently his hands touched a stone that felt familiar.

And it was then that he realized where he was—at the bottom of some kind of an excavation in the ground. Perhaps a well, long since dried up. At any rate, a mass of thorny, wild growth dangled down from the lip.

Leaning weakly against the wall, he renewed his frantic battle with memory. For several minutes he drew nothing but blanks.

And then suddenly it all returned to him with a rush. Like flood waters bursting over the edge of a dam. He stiffened and clenched both fists. In the moment of wild excitement all feeling of pain disappeared.

"I get it," he mumbled. "Must have crashed—where's Bolton?"

Thought of the non-com spurred him into furious action. Shielding his head he grabbed thorny branches with both hands, and tested them. It seemed that the entire pit had caved in on top of him before he found enough dangling trailers to hold his weight.

And then began a slow and torturing pull upward. A dozen times the trailers gave, and he had the sickening expectation of tumbling back down into the pit. But somehow they continued to hold. And after a thousand years of crazy monkey-climbing he succeeded in worming his body up over the lip and onto firm ground. Face downward he lay perfectly relaxed for several moments, pumping air back into his bursting lungs. His brain was spinning a mad dance, and little balls of fire were whirling about before his eyes.

EVENTUALLY, THOUGH, new strength seeped back into his body, and he sat up. All about him was a shadowy mass of immovable objects. He peered at them and made out rocks, tree stumps, and clumps of heavy underbrush. Hardly realizing what he was doing, he glanced down at his wrist watch. The hands showed three hours after midnight.

"Out at least two hours," he mumbled. "But how the hell did I get down there?"

There was no ready answer for that one. Getting to his feet

he stared again at the sky and saw the faint streak of gray light off to his left, marking the east and the beginning of a new dawn. It at least gave him a sense of direction. But, that was all. His exact position could be most anyplace, for all he knew—most anyplace some two hundred and fifty miles behind the Black Invader lines.

"Just a great big help to your country!" he cursed at himself. "Yeah, you can do anything, you—"

He clipped off the sentence short and went rigid. His eyes sweeping helplessly about suddenly became transfixed on a glowing disc off to his right. A disc of glowing yellowish white light beyond a clump of heavy underbrush. Motionless he peered at it, right hand unconsciously fumbling at his bolstered gun under his Black Invader tunic. The disc of light was perhaps fifty feet higher than the ground upon which he stood. It didn't wink, and it didn't move. Just hung there above him against a background of inky darkness.

Clamping down hard on his jangled nerves he started to creep forward stealthily, like a panther stalking its prey. A dozen steps beyond the clump of underbrush the glowing disc disappeared. He stopped short, gun out and body tensed. Not a sound came to his ears. Sky and earth were as silent as the grave.

A few minutes more and he started forward again. And it was then that he realized why the disc had disappeared. He walked smack into the base of a small over-hanging shelf formation on the side of a knoll.

Pausing only long enough to make up his mind, he chose the right and moved off in that direction. Presently he passed the shelf-like formation and came to ground that sloped upward. Looking to the left and up, he again saw the glowing light, but it was elliptical now.

Feeling his way foot by foot he went up the slope, bearing to his left. Perhaps it took him five minutes, or perhaps it was five years, but finally he stopped dead not more than a dozen yards from the light.

"Well, I'll be a—!"

The words hissed off his lips as he straightened up and walked boldly forward. There, in front of him was the crumpled wreckage of his cabin plane. It was a total crack-up loss but he didn't give that fact a single thought.

What caught and held his attention was the center section of the crumpled top wing. Being a part of the cabin ceiling and well braced it was still more or less intact. And in the exact middle was a two-foot disc of glowing phosphorus paint.

The instant he realized what it was, half a dozen gaps in the puzzle picture in the back of his brain filled up immediately.

Hells bells he had been licked right from the very start! Right from the very moment he and Bolton had left the military field at Washington! Those two grease balls that Bolton had been talking to—maybe one of them. But what the hell did it matter?

The point was that some Black agent had painted the disc on the top of the center section, so that any watching Black pilots above could follow his course through the night skies. No wonder that mystery pilot had trailed him, and had been able to attack.

No wonder those rats who had shot him down, had been

able to leap on him at will. Hell, the crate with the glowing disc on the top center section was the target for their bullets. Simple! Simple as hell.

"Yeah, now I know what Curly meant!" he murmured to himself. "Ceiling light on, in a pig's eye!"

Truth smacking home to him from all sides set his blood to a boiling rage. A beginner's trick—but it had nailed him perfectly. True, he couldn't have possibly noticed it at the field. The hangar lights and floodlights blanketed it out. But, it griped just the same. Slipping one over on the Blacks, eh? Nuts! He hadn't even got to first base! And now, here he was, a thousand miles from nowhere with zero-minus ideas on what to do next.

Yet, even with the realization of the bitter truth, he nevertheless went into action.

IT WAS a difficult and tedious job that he set for himself, and half an hour later when it was finished his spirits were a hundred degrees lower. In short, there was not a single trace of Sergeant Bolton in the wreckage.

He had half-expected to find him dead, crushed to a bleeding pulp. But though he had no flashlight, and did not dare risk matches because of the fuel fumes, his search had been thorough, and as he stood staring at the crumpled heap he knew beyond all possible doubt that it contained no body.

And then, suddenly a tantalizing thought trickled into his head. At first he brushed it angrily away, but it kept on coming back to taunt him more and more. Bolton! Was he, after all, a Black?

"Dammit no!" he grated harshly. "Bolton's aces! I know a white man when I—"

He didn't finish the thought. Didn't because a new one suddenly came to him. Fishing in his pockets he pulled out a clip of matches. He hesitated, match-head pressed against the scratcher pad. Lips drawn back in a hard grin he scratched the match.

"When you can't find 'em!" he grunted. "Make 'em try to find you!"

And with that he tossed the lighted flame on the pile of wreckage, spun around on his heel and raced blindly off in the darkness. It was not darkness for long. As a matter of fact, in the space of seconds rugged, shrub-covered countryside became silhouetted by a deep crimson glow. Not pausing to look back, he veered to the left and pounded higher up the slope. At the crest he dove into a towering clump of underbrush, and turned around.

FIFTY YARDS down the slope, and to the right, the remains of the cabin job were blazing fiercely. Great tongues of flame were licking heavenward and lighting up everything for a radius of well over a mile. In almost no time, trees and underbrush within reach of the flames caught fire and added to the gigantic yellow-crimson torch.

Flat on his stomach, Dusty watched it through narrowed eyes. Even where he was he could feel the heat of the flames. But there was no danger of his being trapped, for a slight ground wind was fanning the flames off the edge of the knoll shelf and down the slope.

For a good fifteen minutes the flames raged furiously. In fact they increased in intensity, if anything. For with every passing second another tree or another clump of sun-parched underbrush caught and went up like so much tinder.

The countryside was now virtually bathed in the light of day, and the air was filled with crackling sound. But, no figures came charging into the light cast off by the flames. In fact, the only movement was falling trees and sweeping flames.

And then, suddenly, Dusty's hopes were realized.

From out of a woods, down the slope and to the left, raced three black-uniformed figures. In the same instant his heart both leaped for joy, and chilled with disappointment. The joy was because of the proof that Black forces were located in the area—hence the appearance of three of them. But the disappointment was the continued absence of Sergeant Bolton. If the non-com was still alive—and really an American—he could not possibly have missed the flames and their significance.

Body crouched, eyes hard, he watched the three Blacks run forward until the heat made them stop. Each had a rifle in his hands, and by the motions Dusty knew they were looking for a possible fleeing figure. He grinned and took a tighter grip on his automatic.

Things had not turned out just as he had hoped, but nevertheless a crazy plan was taking shape in his brain. Those three Blacks had undoubtedly come from someplace nearby. It was a cinch that they weren't just wandering around this godforsaken area for their health. Now, if he could just persuade them to do a bit of talking, why—

He ended the thought with a grunt, and started to ease out of the clump of bushes. The Blacks were about sixty yards down the slope, their backs to him and watching the fire. Hugging the ground he eeled from brush clump to brush clump until he was within twenty yards of them. Above the crackle of burning trees he could hear them jabbing their crazy native jargon at each other.

And then he straightened up, and stepped out into the clear. "Drop your guns," he barked. Two of them froze stiff, but the third whirled, his rifle swinging up to his shoulder. And that was his last mistake in this world.

Dusty's automatic spat fire and the Black took a hot slug of steel right square in the middle of his chest. The gun dropped from his hands, then his knees buckled and he folded up on the ground like a deck of cards and lay still.

Without giving him a second look, Dusty started forward, eyes glued on the other two who still stood back to him. They had both dropped their rifles, and looked like two wooden-Indian figures silhouetted against the crimson glow of the flames. Neither of them even moved so much as the fraction of an inch.

"Perfect!" Dusty snapped at them, halting about five yards away, "Now, turn—slowly!"

The one on the right obeyed. He turned around, and then like a flash hurled his body to the right. Down and up streaked his right hand. A revolver barrel glistened, spat flame and sound, and something plucked at Dusty's left shoulder strap. So fast had the man moved that everything he did seemed to happen at the same time.

Perhaps, Dusty's brain registered what was taking place, or perhaps it was simple instinct that made him drop to the ground. At any rate, the action at least postponed his exit from the world.

And the Black had no time, or even a chance, for a second shot. While still dropping, Dusty's gun roared, and the Black's head jerked back as a made-in-the-U.S.A. bullet smashed in through his teeth and out the base of his skull. Like his comrade he folded up on the ground, and that was that.

Bouncing back on his feet like a rubber ball, Dusty took no more chances with the remaining Black who still stood rooted to the ground wooden-Indian style. Going up to the man, he ran his free hand over him, found the holstered gun, and transferred it to his own tunic pocket. Then spinning the man around he held trigger-death about four inches from the Black's nose.

"There's still a few left!" he snapped. "One crazy move, and I make it unanimous! Get me?"

FEAR-GLAZED EYES stared back at him dumbly. Thick lips twitched, and some of the man's native jargon spilled off of them. Dusty cursed inwardly as he realized the situation. The other two knew English and had tried tricks on him. But this one didn't speak the language. Just instinctive warning of danger had made him act as he did. Hells bells—two rats that could be of some use to him stretched out on the ground deader than door nails. And this third rat—a total loss.

"Maybe not at that!" grunted Dusty, as he noticed the man's insignia for the first time.

It was that of a mechanic of the Black Invader Air Force—

crossed props with hawk wings underneath. Heart pounding with new hope, Dusty shot out his free hand and pointed at the insignia. Then he frowned in a puzzled sort of way, waved his hand in a half circle and barked the question.

"Where?"

The Black blinked, licked his lips, and cringed. With a curse Dusty grabbed him and shook him until the man's teeth rattled.

"Where?" he thundered. "Damn you, don't stall. Where? Field—drome—base—where, you tramp?"

The result was to increase the look of stark fear in the Black's eyes. He trembled like a leaf, raised both hands above his head, mumbled something in his native tongue, and shook his head from side to side like a mechanical doll. Dusty gritted his teeth, and tried a new tack.

"Get this then!" he snapped.

With his free hand he pointed at the Black, then at himself, and then went through the motions of a bird flapping its wings in flight. But the Black continued to blink and shake his head. Boiling with rage, Dusty wracked his brain for a way to make the man understand. And then, suddenly, he reached forward and slapped the Black across the bridge of the nose with his gun barrel.

The Black howled, shrank back, and moaned out sounds that had no meaning to Dusty.

"Just making sure you're not fooling!" he grated.

Then as a bright idea struck him, he kept the man covered with his gun, half turned and pointed at the blazing wreck. Then facing the man he gestured questioningly.

DUSTY'S AUTOMATIC SPAT FIRE

"Like that thing!" he said. "Where? You!"

He emphasized the last word by pointing at the man.

And to his great relief, an expression of vague understanding spread over the Black's copperish-tinted face. His lips even slid back in a half smile, and he nodded his head up and down. And then slowly he lowered one of his upraised arms and pointed back toward the woods out of which Dusty had seen him and his two dead comrades appear.

"Swell!" Dusty grinned, nodding his head also. "Now, we're getting to savvy each other. So, let's get going places. Move—you lead, and I'll follow you—and how!"

As he spoke the words he pointed his free hand toward the woods, prodded the Black with his gun, and nodded him forward. The Black caught on instantly, and with hands still in the air he walked along the base of the slope and over toward the patch of woods.

The flames had begun to die down now, all scrub growth and nearby trees having been consumed. And the half-light that marks the mid-point between night and dawn was closing down on all sides.

And so, not trusting the flames to hold out Dusty closed up and practically walked lock-step with the Black, and his eyes didn't leave the man's raised hands for one single instant. As a matter of fact, when they finally entered the woods, Dusty gripped the Black's left shoulder with his free hand, and signified by repeated pressure that any fool tricks would be dealt with accordingly.

WHETHER THE Black was a bright lad who loved life,

or whether Dusty's actions had put the fear of God in him, at any rate he walked stiff as a ramrod through underbrush, even allowing branches to slap against his face, rather than lower his hands and brush them aside. Dusty smiled at the man's perfect obedience, but it was a grim smile of relief and satisfaction. From out of a cockeyed fog it appeared as though he were going to get places at last.

Deeper and deeper into the woods they went, the Black leading and Dusty practically stepping in his footprints. Twice they came upon a narrow path, and the Black followed it for a couple of hundred yards or so. But each time he eventually veered off to one side or the other, and continued to plow straight through the heart of the woods.

And then, without warning, he stopped.

So quick did he stop, that Dusty right behind him almost bowled him over on his face. As it happened he went down on one hand and knee. Instantly on guard, Dusty whipped down his free hand, curled his fingers in the Black's tunic pocket, and jerked him to his feet.

"Didn't I warn you?" he grated, and raised his gun barrel. "You want some of—?"

He stopped as the Black put out pleading hands, and moaned and whined unintelligible sounds. The man's eyes were saucers, and the features of his face were doing all sorts of crazy twitching tricks. Dusty glared at him, and cursed the fact that there was more than one language in the world. And then he realized that the Black was trying to point out something to him on his right.

Eyes riveted on the man, he jabbed his automatic against him hard.

"Just hold it!" he barked. "One move, and good bye!"

The words off his lips, he risked a flashed glance off to the right.

"What the—!"

He hardly heard his own exclamation. Like a man struck suddenly dumb, he stood gaping at a crumpled figure lashed tightly to a tree trunk. The figure's head was sagged down over his chest, concealing the face. And the clothes that he wore could be most anything, they were so ripped and torn and blotched with dirt and some kind of dark, stickish-looking stuff.

Barely conscious that he was dragging the mumbling Black after him, Dusty walked over to the crumpled figure, crooked his gun barrel under the chin and jerked the head up.

And found himself staring down into the blood-caked features of Staff Sergeant Bolton!

CHAPTER 9
THE DEVIL'S BOWL

EVENTUALLY HE pulled his gaze away from the trussed up non-com and glared at the Black in the dim light. The man was grinning, and there was a thoroughly pleased expression on the rest of his face.

For a second, Dusty didn't get it. And then he realized that Bolton tied to the tree trunk was what the Black had thought his pointing to the burning plane had meant. Letting go the

Black, yet keeping a wary eye and his gun on him, Dusty reached down with his other hand and freed Bolton. Then he transferred the stout cord to the Blacks arms and legs.

That done with, he forgot the Black for a moment and knelt down beside Bolton. The non-com was groaning softly. Dusty took him by the shoulders and shook him.

"Out of it, Bolton!" he said in a low but penetrating voice. "Out of it, lad!"

The non-com groaned some more and waggled his head from side to side. On impulse, Dusty slapped him across the cheek and spoke in sharper tones.

"Snap out of it man!"

Bolton's eyes blinked slowly open.

"Eh? What—?"

He sucked in his breath sharply, snarled.

"Go to hell, you bums!" he grated. "There ain't nobody else but me! I'll—"

Dusty clapped his hand over the man's mouth.

"Hold it, lad. It's Ayres! Ayres—do you hear me?"

The non-com slowly stopped blinking. His eyes peered up into Dusty's face, and widened to saucers. Reaching up, he pulled Dusty's hand from his mouth.

"You, skipper?" he gasped. "My God—what?—where the hell did you come from?"

"You all right?" Dusty asked. "Are you hurt?"

The other shook his head.

"No," he said. "Just banged up a bit here and there. But, skipper, where…?"

"Later," Dusty cut him off. "Let's hear your story first. Know how you got here?"

At that moment the Staff Sergeant saw the tied up Black mechanic for the first time. He stiffened, then started to get to his feet. Dusty pulled him down.

"The story, sergeant!" he snapped. "Make it fast. I think we're working against time."

"Well," Bolton began slowly. "After we hit, I woke up with most of the engine in my lap. It was darker than hell, and I couldn't get the old bean working for a couple of moments. Then, I remembered what happened, and I started looking for you. As far as I could tell, your part of the cabin was split clean open. Just like it had been walloped with an axe, or something. Anyway, I couldn't find no trace of you at all. I called your name, but got no answer. And—oh yeah, about then some planes flew over. Probably the guys that got us. And say, on the center section of our ship there was a—"

"Yes, I saw it," Dusty interrupted impatiently. "That's how they were able to pick us out. But, get on with your story."

"And all the time us thinking that we were putting something across!" nodded Bolton. "Can you beat it? Well, anyway, I called you a few times, and then I thought I heard you answer from some place in front of me. I started over that way, and, *zowie*, I walked right off the edge of the world! So help me, I stepped right off into space.

"I thought I'd busted a couple of legs when I hit. Anyway, the next thing I knew, someone is playing a flashlight beam in my face, and a couple of more are tying me up."

"Three of them, eh?" echoed Dusty as Bolton paused.

The non-com nodded and jerked a thumb toward the Black on the ground.

"YEAH," HE said. "Him and a couple of his boy friends— the rats! Well, two of them started to work on me. I mean, asking me where you were. They even said your name, skipper. Well, what they didn't know was swell as far as I was concerned. So I just kept pulling the bluff stuff. Just kept saying that I was solo and lost.

"Well, they got pretty tough. But, hell, I can take it when I have to! Anyway, they didn't learn a damn thing. After awhile they got tired of trying, I guess. They left me with that mug there—the two that was talking to me in English, I mean—and started hunting around the wreck. When they didn't find you— at least I figured it that way—they came back, chinned with themselves a couple of minutes, clipped me a few times for luck, and then started walking me away.

"I remember that just as we were walking into some woods a couple of planes with searchlights came down low. They circled over us a couple of times, and one of the mugs signaled back with his flashlight. Must have been signaling. You know, dot-and-dash stuff?"

Dusty leaned forward eagerly as the non-com paused for breath again.

"Did you see what kind of ships they were, Bolton?" he asked. "Were they Darts, by any chance? You know, center-wing monoplanes?"

The sergeant screwed up his face in deep thought.

"Yeah," he grunted, "I know what you mean, skipper. But, I couldn't say for sure. It was pretty dark, and they didn't come down too low. And besides, their searchlights kind of blinded me, too. Heck, guess I'm not much help, skipper."

Dusty ignored the last. This wasn't the time for patting each other on the back. He half turned and stared speculatively at the trussed up Black mechanic. But after a moment he shook his head and turned back to Bolton.

"Listen, sergeant," he said. "I'm pretty sure that there is a Black drome around here some place. This egg here is an air force mechanic, and so were the other two. Our best bet, in fact our only bet, is to find that drome. When we do, we can begin again from there. Now think hard—do you remember which way those planes flew, after they finished their signaling?"

"Sure," came the prompt answer. "They flew due west."

"How do you know it was west?" Dusty asked him sharply.

"Because I'd already picked out east by the light in the sky," replied Bolton. "In other words, they flew right over the woods those tramps were leading me into. These woods, I guess."

Unconsciously Dusty peered up through the tree branches. To his left the sky was brighter than at any other spot. A moment or two of rapid-fire calculation resulted in the firm belief that although the Black had veered this way and that, his course through the woods had been in a general westerly direction.

"I haven't finished my story, skipper," Bolton suddenly broke in on his thoughts.

"Well?"

"After the ship flew away," the non-com began, "the three

bums with me went into a long pow-wow about something. Don't know what it was, but I gathered the idea that they were plenty worried. Anyway, they went to work on me again, about you. I still played dumb and finally they started booting me through the woods."

Well, after awhile one of them lets out a yip, and we all stop. Behind us, the sky is lighted up by flames. That put them clean off their nuts. They just about went haywire, and before I knew what was happening, one of them slugs me a beaut. And the next thing I realize, I'm looking at you. But what happened to you, skipper?"

Dusty told his story in a couple of sentences.

"Just luck," he finished it off. "The crash hurled me from the cabin and off that little shelf. Probably rolled the rest of the way, and dropped into that hole. Yeah, just luck. But, we're going to need plenty more, Bolton. See if you can stand up."

The non-com got immediately to his feet.

"Oh, I'm O.K., skipper," he grinned. "Can't even feel the clout I got on the dome."

Dusty smiled his admiration. The non-com was probably a great big bunch of pains, as the result of the beating at the hands of the Blacks, but he would bite off his tongue rather than admit it.

"I like 'em tough," Dusty said, getting to his own feet. "Now, let's get going. This Black here doesn't speak the language. We could try sign stuff on him all night and get nowhere. So we'll go it alone. I mean, head west and pray for a break. Damn, almost dawn, too. Oh well, what the hell? Just in case, Bolton, strip him and climb into his uniform. That may help some."

Before Dusty had finished, the non-com was taking the ropes from the Black and peeling off his uniform. The man protested but his protests got him nothing but a few sharp clips on the jaw. Eventually Bolton was garbed as a Black.

"We'd better tie him up again," said Dusty. "Tight enough, anyway, so that it will take him a few hours to get out."

"Don't need to waste the time, skipper," grunted the non-com.

Reaching down his left hand he jerked the Black to his feet, held him at arm's length and then crashed a sledgehammer right-cross against the man's jaw. The Black went down like a felled ox, and didn't even roll over. Dusty started to speak, but Bolton didn't give him the chance.

"Sorry, skipper," he said harshly. "But I feel plenty better. That tramp had it coming. He was the mug who slammed me the most. Guess he'll be hearing birdies for quite awhile."

Dusty simply shrugged and let it go at that. Casting an eye skyward again he rechecked his bearings, handed Bolton the Black's gun he had taken, and started silently off through the woods.

THE HEAVENS grew lighter and lighter, and although that helped some in pushing their way through heavy underbrush, it also served to whet Dusty's nerves to razor edge. Two hours more and the dead line would be reached. Two hours more, and the Hawk would realize that his challenge had been only a stall-bluff. Hell, he probably realized that already! Yeah, probably considered him dead and out of the way for good—and was going ahead with more devilish plans for his stolen C.R.D. unit!

What a mess! What a balled-up, hell of a mess!

"Hey, skipper—do you hear that?"

Bolton's voice pulled Dusty back from the depths of savage and bitter remorse. He stopped and turned around.

"Hear what?" he growled.

The non-com was pointing ahead and to the right.

"That!" he said hoarsely. "That sound—like a waterfall or something."

Dusty strained his ears, heard nothing at first, save the wind in the tree branches above him, then suddenly went rigid. Bolton was right. He could hear a peculiar sound drifting toward him through the dense growth of trees ahead. And it sounded like a waterfall, too. No, not exactly. There was a difference.

It—hell, he'd heard that sound before! Sure, when he came to in that well. It had seemed like breakers pounding on the shore, at first. But later he'd been able to pick out the purring, throbbing undernote—like the roll of countless tom-tom drums.

And the sound he listened to now, was exactly like that. He spun around and plunged forward again.

"That's not a waterfall!" he called over his shoulder. "That's something else—something we're going to find out about, and damn soon!"

Spirits up considerably, he forgot all about fatigue, aches and pains, and went plowing recklessly forward, not caring how much noise he made.

Ahead of him the sound gradually grew louder and louder.

It seemed to come from up in the air somewhere. But though he strained his eyes upward through the tree branches he could see nothing but dawn-flooded skies.

And then presently the woods ended abruptly—cut right off sharp, as though by a gigantic knife. And directly in front of him was a steep ridge, covered with underbrush and circular in formation. He studied it a minute, and listened to the strange sound that now came from beyond the lip of the ridge. At his side Bolton was breathing heavily. Without looking at the man he put out his hand and gripped him by the arm. The other hand he pointed up the ridge.

"Stick close, Bolton," he said. "We've got to see what's behind that. It might be anything, or nothing. But if we run into trouble, use your own judgment—and your gun! Right?"

"Right!" came the low answer. "I'm right with you, skipper!"

Bending over, Dusty darted across a narrow open space and dived into the underbrush. Bolton stuck with him step by step. And then on hands and knees they started eeling up the side of the ridge, and making less sound than a cat walking over a Persian rug.

But when they were within ten or fifteen yards of the top Dusty suddenly froze stiff, shot out his hand and grabbed Bolton. The non-com froze also, and glanced his way. But Dusty wasn't looking at him. Instead he was looking through the underbrush, straight up the ridge—looking at the figure of a Black infantryman, rifle on his shoulder, and pacing slowly back and forth along the crest of the ridge.

"Shall I pop him, skipper?" came Bolton's whispered words. "He's a cinch from here."

Dusty shook his head violently and pushed Bolton's gun hand down.

"Hell no!" he hissed. "There may be others, and a shot will bring them down like a pack of wolves!"

"Yeah, that's so, too," breathed the other. "But what do you figure to do?"

Dusty scowled a moment, pressed his lips together in a thin line. Then suddenly he leaned close to Bolton.

"Wait here, and cover me!" he whispered. "I'm going to try and get him my way. If it goes the wrong way, use your gun and then run for it!"

"But, skipper—?"

"Shut up! Cover me, that's all!"

Flattening out, practically on his stomach, Dusty started to worm up the ten or fifteen dangerous yards. Not once did he take his eyes off the pacing guard, and the gun clutched in his right fist was trained on the man every instant of the time. Eventually, he was hugging the ground beneath some underbrush a bare four feet from a spot where the guard would pass by. At the moment the Black was twenty yards to the right, and back to him.

Virtually holding his breath, Dusty drew his body up to a crouching position inch by inch. Then as the guard turned and started back, he became as motionless as a dead man.

Closer and closer came the guard. Dusty could see his face clearly. The hawkish features were stamped with an expression of utter boredom of an unexciting duty to perform. And the eyes roved lazily about, seemingly noticing nothing.

He half paused a couple of times, and stared dully off and down to his right—in the direction from whence came the strange sound. Because he was hugging the ground Dusty still could not see beyond the lip of the ridge. But that didn't matter to him at the moment. His eyes were glued on the guard. Perhaps later, if—

The guard started walking forward again. He was ten feet from where Dusty crouched. Five feet—now in front of it. And now a step or two past, his back to Dusty.

At that instant, the Yank uncoiled his steel spring muscles and propelled his body through the air. His gun hand was raised above his head; his left hand clawing outward.

PERHAPS THE guard heard him, or perhaps he just sensed immediate danger. At any rate, he whirled like a flash. But, Dusty's movements were even quicker. They were well-nigh invisible.

In one continuous motion he brought the gun barrel down on the Black's skull cap, and crooked his left arm around the man's leathery neck. The guard sighed softly and sank to the ground with Dusty on top of him.

What followed was practically a continuation of the first movement. Arms and legs locked about the prostrate Black, Dusty heaved and rolled them both down into the underbrush. Once hidden he checked the descent, disentangled himself from the Black and got to his hands and knees. Pocketing his automatic he wrenched the Black's rifle from his limp fingers.

He was about to stand up when suddenly the guard moaned faintly and started to raise one hand weakly.

"Tougher than most of them, eh?" gritted Dusty softly.

And with that, he drew his automatic again, held it by the barrel and brought the butt down right square between the guard's eyes.

The half-raised hand dropped automatically and the guard lay still. With a nod of grim satisfaction Dusty took the man's skull cap to replace the one he had lost in the crash, jammed it on his head, and with the rifle at shoulder-slope he stepped boldly up to the top of the ridge and started pacing along its crest.

The first few seconds he devoted to sweeping his eyes along the ridge. At a distance of about a hundred yards on either side of him two more Blacks were doing guard duty. Making sure, from their nonchalant actions, that they had not noticed their comrade dropping out of sight, he turned his eyes to the left.

As he did, a sharp gasp spilled off his lips, and he very nearly stopped dead in his tracks to gape.

The ridge, as he had figured, was circular. In fact it was absolutely round in shape, and served as the rim of a half-mile wide natural crater some three or four hundred feet in depth.

That Dusty saw in a glance. What brought a gasp off his lips, and caused his pumping heart to skip a beat, was what the crater contained.

To begin with, it was flat as a billiard table at the bottom. As a matter of fact, something like the old Yale Bowl at New Haven, Conn. On its south slope were several rows of stone buildings built into the slope so that only the fronts and part of the roofs showed.

And from each front door, which were more like stable doors than anything, a wide ramp slanted downward to the level area. Smaller cross section ramps connected the wide ones, giving the entire southern slope the appearance of a relief map of some boomed-up residential section.

The far-end crater slope contained nothing but a few shrubs and jagged rocks. At its base, however, were three small dome-shaped buildings with "orange peel" doors similar to those used on Zeppelin sheds.

A set of tracks lead out from each shed to a circular platform, and on each platform rested one of the new all metal stratosphere balloons. The bag, which glistened in the dawn light, and was constructed of overlapping and flexible Dural stripping, was semi-inflated. And the ball-shaped gondola, its entrance port open, was fastened to the platform by spring clamps. Close by each platform was a helium tank sunk into the ground so that its top was flush with the surface.

The northern slope and the one on Dusty's side were as bare as the western slope, and he only gave them a quick sweeping glance. In fact, he took in the crater slopes and the stratosphere balloons at the far end with one continuous movement of his eyes. And then they snapped down to the strange sight on the billiard-like floor of the crater. And as he did, his heart pounded against his ribs in wild excitement, and the blood boiled through his veins.

On one side, lined up wing-tip to wing-tip were several Black

Dart monoplanes and three or four cabin planes of Black Invader Unit 10—the Hawk's own personal brood. Several uniformed pilots were lounging against the ships, all seemingly concentrated on an object directly in front of them.

Strange indeed was that object. As Dusty stared at it, his first impression was that he was gazing at some gigantic three-winged dragon fly, poised at the end of a long slotted platform that curved upward at the far end. The three wings were exactly the same in size and shape—two of them in lateral position on either side of a cylinder-shaped cabin, and the third in a vertical position.

Just forward of the wings and the cabin, which was a good ten or twelve feet in diameter tapered down abruptly to a long cylindrical barrel of some two or three feet in thickness. The barrel was about twice the length of the cabin arrangement, and about it were countless coils of steel and copper wire.

SEEING IT from a left rear angle Dusty was unable to tell if the barrel was hollow. But he didn't give that item much thought. What interested him more was the fact that out of the flanging rear end of the strange craft poured the pale white vapor of gas-rocket exhaust. And from the rear end also came the purring and throbbing sound beat.

The craft being some two hundred yards away from him, minute inspection of details was impossible. Never had he seen anything like it before, yet the instant he laid eyes upon it he knew instinctively what it was—the secretly built craft for the stolen C.R.D. unit!

Here was the end of his search. A bit of blind reckoning, and a carload of plain luck had made his C-56 hunch come true. But, what of it? The hunch had come true too late. It didn't take an aeronautical expert to realize that the weird craft was being prepared for flight.

The gas rocket vents were being warmed up to give maximum

driving force for the take-off, and every one of the hundred-odd
Black pilots and mechanics about the field were standing well

clear of the slotted runway. In other words, the craft would take the air at most any minute.

Half of his brain battled with the tantalizing thoughts, the other half still concentrated on the dragon-fly plane. He was now able to see the triple windows of the cabin on the tapering section. And by peering hard he also saw the three-wheel retractable landing gear that was now cranked up into the body.

It was just the reverse of the usual landing gear—two wheels at the rear, and a single landing shock wheel attached forward of the cabin. In short, to facilitate a quick take-off the slotted runway was used, but the craft could be landed on level ground.

And then, suddenly, Dusty cut short his rapid-fire speculation. One of the cabin windows had opened, and a tall black-uniformed figure was legging out onto the take-off runway. He paused there, raised his arm in signal, and a Black mechanic went running over to him. As he reached the platform the tall figure crouched down, and the two of them appeared to engage in some sort of a conversation.

Like molten metal boiling over the lip of a cauldron, stark rage surged up in Dusty. The distance was two hundred yards— two hundred yards between him and that crouching figure on the take-off runway. But it could have been only two feet—less than that, even. One look and he knew, as definitely as the Black mechanic, that the crouching figure was the Black Hawk!

In the back of his mind he had expected the presence of his hated enemy. But now that he was actually seeing him in the flesh, his anger knew no bounds. Oblivious to anything else he stood rigid, narrowed eyes glued on the crouching figure.

The Black Hawk—perhaps, preparing for the bluff meeting with him over the New Hampshire-Canada line. Then again, perhaps preparing for a flight elsewhere. But either way, the devil was preparing for a flight in his terrible death-scattering craft. Preparing for a flight that must not be made!

"Must not be made!"

Dusty repeated the words aloud in savage, gritting tone. He took the rifle from his shoulder and gripped it tightly in both hands. The figure of the Hawk was standing up now. And the mechanic was running back toward the line of Darts. It was obvious that he was going after something, for the Hawk was standing in waiting attitude, doubled fists akimbo on hips.

Brain aflame with berserk anger, Dusty raised the rifle and sighted down the barrel. With icy deliberation he drew a dead-on bead on the Hawk. Then with a curse he lowered the gun.

"No, not that way!" he spat out harshly. "I want him to know it. We'll take that grease-ball first!"

Up went the gun again, but not all the way. He hadn't even started to sight along the barrel, when an inner premonition of danger caused him to turn and glance along the crest of the ridge. There, not thirty yards away, was a Black guard walking rapidly toward him!

CHAPTER 10
THE TORTURE RACK

F OR ONE hellish instant the whole world seemed to drop from under Dusty's feet. His brain screamed for him

127

to swing the rifle and fire, but his arms seemed powerless to move. Yet in the next split second he knew that the rifle butt was at his shoulder, that his eye was sighting down the barrel, and that his finger was curling about the trigger.

And then, as his finger tightened, the advancing Black shook his head, and low words smacked against Dusty's eardrums.

"Nix! Hold it!"

The tiniest part of a fraction of a second more and Dusty would have fired. Yet he didn't, and in that space of time he relaxed, dropped the rifle and glared at Sergeant Bolton walking toward him.

"You damn fool!" he hissed. "I might have killed you!"

The non-com, rifle at the slope, grinned.

"Chance I had to take, skipper," he said out the corner of his mouth. "Saw what you did, and tried it myself. Didn't hanker to hug them bushes all day. The other egg won't be up for a long time—so chances of bumping into somebody are less, see?"

Dusty didn't answer. He was still shaking inwardly from the close call. One instant more and he would have fired—killed a man who was really trying to help him, and attracted the attention of every Black in the crater, to say nothing of the half-dozen guards patrolling the rest of the ridge.

"What's that thing down there, skipper?"

"What we're after!" he snapped. "Start patrolling, you fool!" he added. "They've got eyes down there. Go fifty yards and turn. When we meet I may have a plan worked out. Get!"

Turning his back on the man, Dusty started to slouch along the crest of the ridge. But though his movements were lazy and slow, his brain was racing over at maximum speed. In the excitement of seeing the C.R.D. plane he had forgotten all about Bolton. And now, the appearance of the man simply added to the problem.

The C.R.D. ship must not take off—regardless of what happened, Bolton, the Hawk, himself, or anybody else did not matter.

Yeah, but how in the name of heaven could he stop it? Kill the Hawk? Maybe—personal desires were out, now. He'd never shot a man, even a Black, in the back. But, this was no time for chivalry and so-called war sportsmanship. However, the target wasn't such a hot one. Only two hundred yards to be sure. But the rifle he had was not a sniper's long-range rifle.

And besides, the Hawk was half hidden by the right lateral wing of the plane. One shot was all he'd be allowed, probably. One shot, and then hell would bust loose. But maybe Bolton—

He cut the thought off short, turned around and started walking back. The non-com had already paced his fifty yards and was coming toward him. A minute or so later they were ten yards apart.

"Ears back, Bolton!" Dusty clipped out softly. "We've got to stop that ship from taking off. That's the Hawk beside it. Get as near the Black on your side of the ridge as you can—and shoot him.

"Pick him right off. I'll do the same to the lad on my side. Got to be done. Then concentrate on that ship, and anyone near it. If we both pop from different angles, it may hold up the parade long enough for me to do something else. Maybe curtains—but it's our only bet. We must keep that ship on the ground. Got it?"

"Got it!" answered the other quietly.

"Good lad," grunted Dusty, as he turned. "Luck!"

WITHOUT LOOKING back, he marched along the crest of the ridge toward the nearest Black guard who stood leaning on his rifle less than a hundred yards away. With each step Dusty's sense of fair play boiled up in protest, but he savagely quelled it, and walked grimly forward.

And then finally, when he was within thirty yards of the Black, he snapped up his rifle and pulled the trigger. The guard threw up his arms and toppled over like a ten-pin.

"Sorry, rat!" Dusty grunted as he hurled himself down on his stomach. "But, it had to be that way."

Hugging the ground, he squirmed around, put the rifle to his shoulder and drew a bead on the C.R.D. ship. Because of the vertical wing he could not see the Black Hawk. Regardless of that, though, he squeezed the trigger and slapped a steel slug down at the plane.

At almost the same instant he heard Bolton's rifle crack on the opposite side of the crater. But he didn't bother to look that way. He simply breathed a prayer that the non-com had got his man, and drew a bead on a running Black mechanic. The man was running toward the C.R.D. plane. As Dusty's rifle crashed out sound the man ran two steps more, did a funny little dance, and then went sprawling on his face.

By now, the bowl of the crater was a scene of wild excitement. Figures were running about in all directions, and the air clattered with rifle fire. Thrown into a momentary panic the Blacks were shooting wildly. Out the corner of his eye, Dusty saw a guard pounding along the ridge crest toward him. In one flash movement he swung the rifle around and fired—and the guard seemed to do a back-flip before he melted into the ground.

Swing front again, he let out a bellow of rage. The Black Hawk had leaped down off the run-way platform and was racing madly over toward the line of Dart planes.

"Take it, then!" howled Dusty. "Take it!"

One-two-three-four hunks of steel he slammed down at the running figure, and all four of them kicked up little puffs of dirt at the man's feet..

He cursed as he realized that the rifle sights were set low, and took aim again for a point about two feet above the Hawk's bobbing head. Then he pulled the trigger—and a split second later he shouted with joy.

Like magic the Hawk's right leg seemed to fold under him. Unable to check his speed he slumped down and went spinning head over heels, like a rag doll hurled down a flight of stairs by some petulant youngster. As a matter of fact, the cloud of dust kicked up by the skidding figure completely, hid it for a second or two.

But as the dust cleared, and a group of Black started running toward it, Dusty swung his rifle toward them.

"Let the rat suffer a bit!" he snarled, and jerked the trigger.

And it was then that his heart went sliding down into his boots. The firing pin clicked forward and that was all. The clip of eight rounds had been used up.

Dusty groaned, then cursed himself for not having grabbed extra clips from the belt pouch of the original owner of the rifle. Across the crater bowl the almost continuous rapid fire from Bolton's rifle told him that the non-com had had more sense.

On impulse, Dusty rolled over and started toward the guard he had killed, to get his extra clips—and then checked himself as a seemingly better idea flashed across his brain.

The Blacks were concentrating their return fire on Bolton. Not a single shot was coming his way now. God, if only Bolton could keep them occupied—

With a curse, Dusty slung the rifle to one side, and rolled his body off the crest of the ridge and down in the underbrush. Checking himself, he pulled his automatic and went creeping down the slope. When he was almost at the bottom, he turned sharp right and started around the base of the ridge.

The rifle and machine-gun fire was by now making the very atmosphere tremble with its clattering sound. It seemed to Dusty that a hundred fingers must be pulling triggers. A hundred fingers against one of Bolton's. Bolton—God bless him!

For a moment Dusty was possessed with the desire to go back and fight it through with the non-com, side by side. But, his better judgment killed the desire almost as soon as it was born. No time, now, for heroics. Bolton was doing his job. And it was up to him to do his. Together—they might last perhaps ten minutes. Apart—

"It's our only chance," murmured Dusty. "Our only chance, and I'm counting on you!"

Presently, the firing died down, then ceased altogether. To Dusty it was as the tolling of a death-knell for Bolton. Crouching under the heavy brush he strained his ears, hoping against hope to hear the firing break out anew. But not a single sound of a shot crashed out. Nothing but silence. And as he realized that, he started violently. It meant that the gas rocket powerplant of the C.R.D. ship had been shut off. Maybe—

He blurted the thought out loud.

"Maybe Bolton smacked it a bit!"

WITH THE wild hope that such might be the truth, he gave up the plan of following the base of the ridge further, and started creeping up the slope. Eyes straining toward the lip, he eeled up foot by foot, and finally reached the crest.

Body pressed against the ground, he darted a quick glance to the right and to the left. There was not a single Black guard in sight. And then as he looked across the crater bowl he saw the black-uniformed figures swarming up the slope. At the top stood three figures; two of them holding up between them the limp body of the third figure.

Distance didn't matter. Dusty knew instantly who the third figure was, and a bitter groan slid off his lips.

"Thanks, buzzard!" he murmured. "I'll make good for your sake—or join you!"

Tearing his eyes from the group he looked down the slope on his side. He was directly above the rows of stone-and-metal-roofed buildings built into the side of the slope. Directly across from them was the long, slotted take-off runway, curved up at one end, and with the C.R.D. ship poised at the other end.

From this new angle he suddenly saw that the craft was really a four-winged affair. The fourth wing corresponded with the top vertical wing, only it extended downward into the slot. Guideways on its surface indicated that it could be pulled up into the cabin part during a landing.

Incidentally, no vapor was spewing out from the flanged rear section. And as Dusty realized that his surmise had been correct, he instinctively nodded with grim satisfaction and hope. Perhaps the craft was not damaged by bullets, but at least its power was shut off, which meant that a take-off was not a thing of the immediate future.

The Blacks had captured Bolton—perhaps killed the brave fellow—but they must realize that two, and not just one rifle, had been popping at them. And realizing that, they would undoubtedly concentrate on hunting down the owner of the other trigger finger. In other words, Dusty knew that his wild and fervent prayer was being answered. He had gained a brief respite in time—and time was the one thing that mattered now above all else. With time on his side there was the chance for him to washout all of his unconscious blunders of the last twenty-four hours, and really do something that was helpful to the cause for which he battled.

Snake-like, eyes darting in all directions, he started to wiggle down the slope toward the first row of buildings. Whether barracks, experimental laboratories, or what, he did not know. Nor did he care for the moment. One thought was in his mind.

DUSTY PLUNGED THROUGH THE DOOR

It was the thought of an old adage—"The best place to hide anything is to place it right under the searcher's eyes."

And that was what he planned to do—to hide himself right under the Blacks' eyes. His uniform was that of the enemy. He wore one of their skull caps, and unless he was confronted face to face, there was a chance that his copperish tinted skin would give him the break he needed—the chance to reach the C.R.D. ship. And when he did—

He let the rest die in his brain. He had reached the last of the underbrush. From now on he would have to show himself, walk boldly down in the open. Hesitating a minute, he fixed his eyes on the opposite side of the crater bowl. The crest where Bolton had been was black with Invader uniforms. And then as his eyes lowered to the C.R.D. ship, with no sign of a figure near it, he jammed the automatic into its holster, sucked in his breath and started brazenly down the hill.

Passing between two of the buildings, he had the sudden, crazy belief that the windows were jammed with cruel faces staring out at him. And in spite of himself he raised his eyes and stared at them—and heaved a shaky sigh. There were windows in the buildings, right enough. But not a single Hawk-featured face was pressed against them.

That helped a bit, but not too much. Nerves still jangling slightly he walked past the top row of buildings, mounted up on a cross ramp and started along it toward one of the main ramps leading down to the flat bottom of the crater. Past three buildings he went, dully conscious of a peculiar smell in his nostrils. It was something like burning rubber, only less pungent.

Perhaps, it was more like the smell of smoking sulphuric acid. Maybe not that. He was simply dully conscious of the smell, and as the major portion of his brain concentrated on being on the alert, a tiny corner occupied itself with the strange smell that, incidentally, seemed to come from no particular direction.

And then, suddenly, his entire brain focused on one thing. A Black mechanic racing down the opposite slope and across the bottom of the crater!

Wildly, Dusty glanced about. But there was no place of hiding for him to duck into. And the man was heading straight for the slanting ramp upon which he stood. He automatically jerked a hand to his gun, but snapped it down almost instantly and breathed a curse. To shoot would ruin everything. And it was too late to do anything else. The man was headed straight for him. He could do nothing but chance it and trust to luck.

Five seconds. Five short, fleeting seconds during which Dusty was rigid with apprehension. And then, without even flinging him a side glance, the Black guard raced past up the ramp and shouldered in through the stable-like doors of one of the buildings. For a moment as reaction set in Dusty's head whirled, but in a flash it cleared, and he continued down the ramp.

That is, he continued for perhaps half a dozen steps.

And then a mighty roar of rage brought him up short. A roar of rage coming from the building behind him. A split second later there came the crack of a revolver shot, and a human voice cried out in mortal pain. And as it died to the echo, a harsh voice blasted out sound in the jargon of the Black Invaders.

The voice went through Dusty like a knife. It was a voice he would never forget. Others might be like it, but not exactly like it. Only one man on the face of the globe had a voice like that. And half an hour, or more, ago that man had cartwheeled over in a cloud of dust as a hunk of steel slapped into his rotten hide!

Caught between the wild impulse to plow in through those stable doors and finish the job, and an equally wild impulse to make a desperate break for the C.R.D. ship, Dusty stood rigid.

But a moment later he had no chance to do either. The doors of the building slammed open and a handful of Blacks came charging out. Voices roaring unintelligible sounds, they pounded down the ramp right past him, and on across the field. Through startled eyes Dusty watched them go scrambling up the opposite slope to where a group of their comrades still stood on the crest.

"Now what?"

The words from his lips were but a soft murmur, but the very sound of them made him jump involuntarily. Savagely he clamped down on his nerves and battled with himself for decision. The plane, or the Hawk? A chance for one—not both. He could run up the ramp, and perhaps nail the Hawk, who was still in that building. The Invader ace had not been one of the shouting group that raced past him. Or he could make a break for the plane. The Blacks on the opposite ridge crest were all coming down now in a body. But they were an equal distant from the C.R.D. ship as he.

And at that instant a defiant voice speaking English blasted all thought of the C.R.D. plane from his mind.

"Go to hell, you rotten, murdering vulture! Go to hell and fry in your own grease! I'll be damned if I'll tell you!"

Recognition of that defiant voice swept through Dusty with tornado fury. It had come from the lips of General Horner, Chief of U.S. Intelligence! Like a man awakening from a vivid dream he remembered that the general had been captured along with the C.R.D. unit. So much had happened since then, that he had completely forgotten. But now—

He turned, jerked his automatic from its holster, and started up the ramp toward the doors of the building. One of them was partly open, and through it came the harsh voice of the Black Hawk.

"It will not be pleasant, general, I promise you. Far better that you tell me the code signal, so that I can communicate with your son. Nothing can save him, regardless of whether you tell me or not. Now, what is it?"

Dusty was almost at the door when General Horner spoke again.

"You can still go to hell, you dirty killer!"

The sentence was immediately followed by a moan of pain. A moan of pain that Dusty knew instinctively came from Horner's lips. He hesitated but a split second, then hurled himself through the partly opened door. In one lightning-like glance around he took in every detail of the picture inside.

The room was square with a door at the far side. Near the door, seated in a chair, *sans* tunic and shirt, was the Black Hawk. The man's left side was covered with bandage. In front of him and about five feet away was General Horner. The Intelligence

139

chief was lashed spread-eagle to metal framework that could be increased or decreased in size. Behind the framework, one talon-like hand grasping the crank-handle fitted to a set of ratchet gears, was a Black soldier. And to the left, fastened to the wall was a complete broadcasting and receiving radio panel. The red contact wave-length bulb was glowing.

All that Dusty saw in the flicker of an eyelash. And then he saw the Black soldier's right hand streaking for a gun. Half spinning, Dusty slapped his own gun across his chest and fired. The Black fired at almost the same instant, but his bullet plowed into the floor. The gun dropped from his fingers as he fell over backwards and hit the floor stiff as a tree-trunk.

In almost the same motion, Dusty swung all the way around and pointed the barrel of his gun straight at the Hawk's bare chest. The Black had not moved. Like a man of stone, he sat gapping at Dusty, his cruel, jet-black eyes wide with a look of utter disbelief.

"Good lord—you, Ayres!"

It was General Horner who gulped out the words. Dusty didn't even look toward him. He kept his eyes fastened on the Hawk, stuck back one foot and kicked the door shut. Then backing up to it he fumbled with one hand, found the inside locking bolt and rammed it home. Then, he grinned at the Hawk.

"Not exactly expecting me, eh?"

The sound of his voice caused the Black to relax.

"Frankly, no," he said in a low voice. "But, now that you are here, I've been saved a lot of trouble. I've been wanting to meet you, you know."

"So I heard—or rather, read," nodded Dusty.

As he spoke he walked over close to the Hawk, bent down and peered at him hard.

His eyes searching the man's face saw the tiny cut on the lower lid of the right eye. It was the one marking that distinguished the real Black Hawk from all of his pinch hitters. With a grim nod Dusty straightened up.

"Really, you, this time, eh?" he grunted. "Swell! Now just sit tight, while I get General Horner off this damn rack. No—try anything you want. It's the final payoff this time and I'd just as soon plug you now as after I've given you a taste of your own medicine."

The Hawk did not snarl, nor was there any trace of fear in his voice he spoke.

"You forget, my dear captain, that there are over a hundred of my men outside, any one of whom would love to take your life. I suggest that you surrender quietly. It will be better for you in the end."

Dusty chuckled, backed over to the frame work, and with his free hand unwound the gears so that all tension was taken off General Horner's spread eagled arms and legs. The senior officer groaned with relief. And as Dusty unsnapped the clamps that held him, the man mumbled thanks and rubbed his raw wrists and ankles.

"Sit down and rest, sir," said Dusty, without looking at him. "I'll be with you in a minute."

Eyes still on the Hawk he walked over to his chair.

"I guess," he gritted, "that what you say is quite correct. Anyone of your rats outside would love to do this and that to me. But it's kind of tough that they are outside and you are inside. How's the shoulder? Not bad shooting for the distance was it? Too bad my slug didn't go about three inches farther over."

The Hawk smiled, and nodded his compliments.

"I will return the favor in due time, captain," he said.

"That'll be nice," grinned Dusty. And then in steely tones. "Up, bum! General Horner's had enough for awhile. Now, it's your turn to show us how this thing works. Up—or must I tap you one?"

The Black's eyes slithered from Dusty's face to the rack and back again. He licked his lips and swallowed.

"Yup, you've guessed it," Dusty cut in on his thoughts. "I've seen you pull some sweet torturing stunts in months gone by—so now I'm going to see how you like it! Up, damn you!"

As he spoke the last, Dusty reached out his free hand and jerked the Hawk to his feet. The Black groaned with pain, and clamped a hand over his bandaged side.

"Your tough luck," Dusty bit off. "Now, back up. There, that's the idea."

The Hawk, his eyes now blazing with hate, backed up until he was against the rack. In quick movements, Dusty clamped his wrists and ankles against the cross pieces, then darting around to the handle he turned it just enough to straighten out the man's muscles. Then, pocketing his automatic he went over and sat in the Hawk's chair.

"Now, general," he grinned at the Intelligence chief, "help yourself. I believe the rat was trying to get something out of you?"

General Horner had by now regained full control of his tongue. He bounded over and grasped Dusty's hand.

"Thanks—thanks more than I can say!" he blurted out. "But we're trapped in here, Ayres. He's right about there being others outside. We can't possibly hope to shoot our way through them. But, how in the name of God did you get here? I thought you were going to M-29?"

M-29 again!

Dusty scowled questioningly at the other.

"What made you think that, sir?" he asked sharply.

The General half turned and pointed over toward the radio panel on the wall. Then he pointed at the Hawk.

"He heard you talking with Brooks. I heard you, too. Brooks said that he'd see you later at M-29. That's why this devil has been torturing me. He wanted Brooks' secret code number. He was going to fake you and find out why Brooks was to meet you there."

Dusty shrugged and gazed absently at the dead Black on the floor, and at another dead Black in the far corner—the one, probably, who's cry of pain he had heard when out on the ramp.

"There's a lot of things that don't make sense yet, sir," he said, getting to his feet. "And that's one of them. But, just hold it a second."

He started over toward the Hawk when Horner grabbed him.

"But, you don't understand, Ayres! They've been calling you for the last hour. And I'm afraid they're heading for this place. At least they intimated that in their last message."

Dusty stopped short, and whirled.

"They?" he echoed sharply. "Who? What the devil are you talking about, general?"

Horner gestured wildly.

"Agent 10 and Brooks!" he shouted, again pointing toward the radio panel. "They're in the air. Been calling for you for an hour!"

Hardly had the Intelligence chief ceased talking, when the speaker unit on the wall crackled out sound.

"Calling two-four-two! Calling two-four-two. Meet me over M-29 as soon as possible. Emergency!"

Dusty stared at the speaker unit. It was the voice of Curly Brooks calling him on his secret wave-length reading. Behind him the Hawk chuckled harshly. He spun around and glared at the man.

"Yeah?" he clipped out.

"Your friend is very stupid indeed," said the Black quietly. "I suggest that you look at the station directional finder dial, captain."

As Dusty's eyes leaped to the dial he groaned in spite of himself.

"You see, captain?" the Hawk's voice drummed in his ears. "Your friend is south of this area—at least five hundred miles from M-29. The fool!—does he not realize that we know he is getting nearer and nearer to this area? Yes—and a most unusual reception awaits him, and his passengers!"

CHAPTER 11
CLIPPED WINGS

D USTY STOOD perfectly still for perhaps fifteen seconds. Then he stepped close to the Hawk.

"Meaning just what?" he snapped.

The Black made as though to shrug, but his tightened arms and legs prevented the gesture.

"You surprise me, captain," he said. "Haven't you guessed it? Your friend, Lieutenant Brooks, thinks that he is very clever. Since he first spoke with you last night, he has been trying to make us believe that M-29 is your destination. But, you see, we knew where you were headed. And we also know that Lieutenant Brooks and this Agent 10—not having heard from you for hours—are really trying to sneak into this area and find you. All that we know, captain—eh, General Horner?"

Like a man caught helpless between two fires, and not knowing which way to turn, Dusty simply looked at General Horner. The Intelligence chief nodded.

"He's telling you the truth for once, Ayres," he said. "The devils have been checking by radio for hours. I heard the reports coming in myself. God knows why they haven't found them by now. That's why this rat wants Brooks' code signal. He wants to pull them into an exact spot so that his vultures can jump

145

on them. Either that, or he planned to do it with his C.R.D. plane."

Dusty said nothing. But inwardly he cursed Curly Brooks to Timbuktu and back again. He could guess exactly what had happened. Curly had undoubtedly got in touch with Agent 10, and wormed the story out of him. And then they'd decided to do something on their own hook. Curly's idea, probably. The first item had been an insane plan to make the Blacks think that he was at M-29. And now—just as the Hawk had said—not having heard from him they were highballing straight for C-56, blissfully thinking that the Blacks were fanning vacant air over M-29.

"The dummies! My God—!"

Dusty shut up as he realized he was speaking out loud. The Hawk chuckled some more.

"Exactly, captain," he purred softly. "It makes the situation very delicate, doesn't it? You and the good general are already here. So is the sergeant pilot who accompanied you. Unfortunately—rather, fortunately for him, he was taken alive. And very soon Lieutenant Brooks and Agent 10 will also be our guests. What is the phrase? Ah yes—a grand slam!"

Dusty hardly listened to the man. He did, however, note the fact that Bolton was still alive. And for that, he was truly thankful. But what next? What was the best move to make? For the moment he was safe. Four thick stone walls protected him and General Horner. But hell, Curly and Jack Horner were flying blindly into a perfect trap. To warn them over the radio would simply be telling every station listening in just where he was. They might guess the rest and in no time pile down and literally fill the C-56 crater with men and guns. Then what? True, if he died so would the Hawk die. He'd make damn sure of that. But—

At that moment, as though the man had actually read his thoughts, the Hawk broke in upon them.

"Very complicated, captain! And to use the phrase that has so often come from your own lips—'My life means very little. There are many others to take my place.' Yes, very complicated indeed. The Black Hawk dies—but so does the great Captain Ayres, the great General Horner, the famous Agent 10, one Lieutenant Brooks, and an insignificant sergeant pilot. And— one of the most ingenious war weapons of all time remains with the Black Invaders, conquerors of all the world!"

Dusty stood looking at him, as word by word the bitter truth smacked against his ear-drums. Once he had believed the Hawk to be yellow at heart. But it didn't seem that way now. The Black seemed to know that death was close, yet it did not change him a single bit. He was still possessed of his distorted sense of merciless triumph.

And then, suddenly, Dusty burst out laughing.

"A neat little speech!" he hurled at the Black. "And you were damn close to being right. But a ten-year-old kid could put a fast one over on your bums. Listen how it's done."

Ignoring the detaining hand that General Horner reached out, Dusty walked over to the radio panel, swung on maximum volume power, and spun the wave-length dial to the emergency reading. Then, looking at the Hawk, he put the transmitter tube to his lips.

"Urlycay amscray outhsay ontopray! Urlycay amscray outhsay ontopray!"

As the last left his lips he snapped off the set, and walked back to the chair. A frown creased the Hawk's brows, and his black eyes were wide with puzzled confusion. General Horner's expression was much the same. He leaned toward Dusty.

"Good Lord, Ayres!" he cried. "What the devil was all that gibberish?"

Dusty grinned at the Hawk.

"That was school-days stuff, tramp," he said. "We used to call it talking in pig-Latin. To translate for you, I said—Curly scram south pronto! Maybe you don't get the slang, but I'm sure you get the idea. Right?"

The Hawk said nothing, but the look of hate in his eyes increased in intensity. General Horner gasped, and muttered something that Dusty didn't catch. He didn't try to. He simply leaned toward the Hawk.

"And now we'll go over the last part of the act," he said. "Some of your bums will be along soon. Maybe they're bringing my pal, the sergeant, over for you to work on. Is that what you sent those eggs tearing out of here for?"

The Black still remained silent. And his very silence answered Dusty's question. He grinned and nodded.

"Thought so," he said. "Now, listen carefully. When they bang on the door, you tell them to send their prisoner in alone, see!"

The Hawk's lips curled in a snarl.

"You fool!" he grated. "Do you think I will do that? I'll order them to storm this place and kill you both. Oh yes, you may kill me—but you, too, will die, Captain Ayres. And don't forget that plane out on the field. It will still belong to us. And in time, hundreds more will be constructed and—"

He didn't finish the rest. Sliding up to him, Dusty whipped him across the mouth with the back of his hand.

"You talk too much!" he bit off. "Now, just calm down and listen to me. You're going to do just as I tell you. You know, I used to have a certain sense of fair play—a sort of sportsmanship. But since I've been tangling with you and your rotten skunks I've lost all that. And right now, I'm going to play the game your way!"

With a lightning like movement, Dusty shot out his hand and gave the crank handle a full turn. As the rack pulled the Hawk's legs and arms outward he howled with pain, and great beads of sweat oozed out on his wrinkled forehead. His jaw sagged open, and his thick lips quivered. Dusty stared at him coldly. "Your way! Get the idea! Sure, you're going to die. But, not quickly, like you figure. No, a bullet is too fast. However, I'm going to give you your choice. And I mean this—so help me! You can do as I say, and go out fast with a hunk of lead in your thick skull. Or you can get funny, and go out your way—first an arm, then a leg, then the other arm. Then a little rest while I revive you, if you've fainted. Yup—I'm going to play the game your way!"

As Dusty stopped talking, the Black groaned and the features of his face twisted with pain. Grabbing the handle Dusty unwound it half a turn. A rasping sigh of relief came from the Hawk's lips.

"Feels better that way, doesn't it?" the Yank clipped at him. "Now, as I was saying—when your rats arrive, tell them to send the prisoner in alone. And then tell them to go and wait for you in the mess hall. All of them, see? That's the last building down to the left. I spotted it, and I'll be watching to see if they go there. Now, that's all there is to it. Very simple, if you're a wise lad. But, it will be very tough if you get funny. I'll—"

Dusty cut himself off short. Feet were pounding on the ramp outside, and there was a mingled growl of voices. With a quick movement Dusty shoved the framework against the wall, and then pulled his automatic.

"I don't know your lingo!" he breathed fiercely at the Hawk. "But, by God, one funny move and you'll wish you'd never been born. See—I've got my hand on the crank. And the General and I can hold them off for quite awhile. That door's heavy, you know."

At that moment a fist pounded on the door, and a harsh voice said something in Black Invader jargon. Dusty swept his eyes around to General Horner's face.

"You!" he whispered. "Let just one man in, then slam the door. Take one of those guns, and be ready to use it."

The Intelligence chief simply nodded, scooped up a gun from one of the dead Blacks, and went over to the door. Hand on the bolt, he stood watching Dusty. The pilot had his eyes glued on the Hawk.

"Speak your piece!" he whispered. "Speak your piece—and

God help you!" The features of the Black's face twitched and quivered violently. He licked his lips and glared venomously at Dusty. The Yank returned it with an agate glare and moved the crank handle half an inch.

"Say it, damn you!" he hissed. "Say it!"

A long tensed second of silence was suddenly punctuated by continued pounding on the door. The Hawk swallowed hard, gave Dusty a final look, then parted his lips and poured out words in his native tongue. As he stopped, Dusty nodded at General Horner and steeled himself for instant action. The Intelligence chief, his face an ashy white, hesitated a second then slid the bolt back and slowly opened the door.

As it swung open Dusty's heart pounded against his ribs and his whole body became electrified with nerve quivering excitement. His eyes saw nothing but the door swinging open a foot, and the gun in his hand was trained dead on it. For one split second the entire universe seemed to pause and wait.

And then a black-uniformed figure came hurtling through the opening.

The instant it was inside and sprawling onto the floor, General Horner slammed the door shut and rammed the locking bolt home. And in that same instant also, Dusty leaped across the room and bent over the sprawled-out figure. Rage-filled eyes blazed up at him. They were the rage-filled eyes of Sergeant Bolton.

The non-com's lips curled back in a snarl, and then as though by magic his whole expression changed to one of blank, unbelievable astonishment. Lunging up on one elbow, he made queer gurgling sounds in his throat. Presently they became half gasped words.

"Skipper—skipper—you? How—what? My God, is this a cockeyed dream, or—?"

"It's real," Dusty cut him off. "Can you stand up? Did they hit you?"

"Stand up?" echoed Bolton, doing that very thing. "Hell yes, sure I'm O.K.! Those tramps weren't exactly gentle, but—"

He stopped short as his saucer-like eyes spotted General Horner and the Black Hawk for the first time. He automatically stiffened, clicked his heels and saluted the Intelligence chief.

"General Horner!" he breathed in a gulping sound. "What is all this—?"

Dusty didn't hear the rest. Once sure that Bolton was all right, he slid over to the door, pulled back the bolt, and eased it open the fraction of an inch. Eye glued to the crack he looked out and to the left. About a hundred yards away Black officers and mechanics were walking along the side of the field toward a large stone building near the western end of the crater. A few others were approaching it from the other side. Dusty grinned, and twisted so that he could look directly across the crater. There wasn't a soul near the line of Black Darts and cabin observation ships.

Closing the door and bolting it again, Dusty turned and walked over to the Hawk.

"Guess you've got a brain after all," he said. "As a reward, I'll give you a rest from that thing."

Unwinding the crank he released the clamped wrists and ankles. Legs having been almost stretched to the snapping point, the Hawk was unable to walk. He would have crashed down on his face had not Dusty grabbed him and let him drop into a chair.

"Just sit tight for a spell," Dusty grunted at him. "Just sit tight—and keep your eye on this gun I'm lugging around."

The Hawk made no comment. He was too far gone to talk. Cruel features strained with pain, he slumped back and stared dully at the ceiling. Dusty eyed him coldly without a single tremor of pity, and then sidled over to where Horner and Bolton stood gaping at him questioningly.

"Luck was with us that time, Ayres," the Intelligence chief grunted. "But, I'd keep that devil trussed up. He doesn't deserve any pity. And—"

"And he's not getting any," Dusty cut him off. "But I had to take him down, sir. I want you to climb into his clothes. I see that his tunic is over there in the corner. His skull cap, too. It's another break for us that you're about the same build."

"Climb into his clothes?" echoed Horner incredulously. "Good heavens, you don't mean that—?"

Dusty's quick gesture shut him up.

"Hold it, sir, please! We're going to do this thing my way. Now, I want you to get into the Hawk's clothes, act as though you'd been shot in the side—you know, sort of bent over—and then you and Bolton here are to walk over to one of those cabin planes. Bolton—the controls are the same as in most of our ships. You won't have any trouble. Take off and fly the General straight back to our side of the lines. Don't stop for anything, see? If you run into any of our ships, tell them who you are by radio. But—go straight through at maximum revs! Understand?"

The non-com licked his lower lip and half nodded.

"Yes, sure, skipper!" he blurted out. "But what about you? I don't want to leave you here, and—"

"Never mind about me!" Dusty snapped. "I gave you orders. Orders that are to be obeyed without question."

"Yes sir!" replied Bolton humbly. "Very good, sir."

But General Horner was far from satisfied.

"I don't agree, Ayers," he said bluntly. "I'll be damned if I see any reason why you should stay here. Good Lord, man, you've pulled enough miracles as it is. I insist that you come along with us. I won't let you stay here."

Dusty cursed inwardly, fixed the other with a steely gaze.

"I don't intend to stay here!" he bit off. "You're missing the point completely—the C.R.D. ship. I'm flying that back to the States! Now please change clothes with him."

Horner nodded, and started over to the Black.

"Oh," he said weakly. "Yes, you're quite right. I had forgotten about that. Sergeant—give me a lift with this."

Dusty toying with his gun, stood watching while the two of them stripped the Hawk of his uniform. He half expected the Black to put up a battle. But in that he was disappointed. Without saying a word, in fact without even changing the half-groggy, listless expression on his face, the Hawk silently submitted. And presently General Horner was fully garbed from head to foot in the uniform of the ace of Black Invader pilots. Dusty gave him an approving nod.

"Not bad at all, sir," he grinned. "But, I suggest that both of you keep your faces down as you walk across the field. And, for God's sake, don't run. Walk quickly. I'll watch you from here. If I fire two quick shots—run for it. O.K., Bolton, I'm counting on you again, buzzard."

"But, I thought you said—" began General Horner.

"Later," Dusty interrupted. "Now don't argue, sir. You two getting safely into the air will help me more than anything else. So please get going."

The Intelligence chief gave him a long searching look. Then he shrugged and turned toward Bolton.

"Alright, sergeant," he got out gruffly. "No sense in arguing with a madman, I suppose."

Dusty grinned, and saluted.

"Thank you, sir. Luck to you both!"

Horner snorted, slapped the bolt back, and pulled open the door.

CHAPTER 12
THE TRAP OPENS

KEEPING ONE eye on the listless Hawk, Dusty watched his two friends go through the door and start slowly down the ramp. For one wild second he was tempted to slug the Hawk and go with them. But he savagely killed the urge. There was no sense in forcing his luck. It was far better for the two of them to go it alone. Any Black who might be watching probably wouldn't think so much about two men walking over to the other side of the crater. But, if they saw some one get into the C.R.D. ship, then they might get suspicious. And besides, slugging was not the way out for the Hawk. No, not by a damn sight. This was the final show-down, and it was going to include the works from A to Z—and then some!

Standing well back from the opening, yet in a position to see the mess building as well as his friends, Dusty virtually held his breath in tingling suspense. Both Horner and Bolton were playing their parts to perfection, but in the tenseness of the situation their progress seemed hellishly slow to Dusty. He wanted to yell at them to get a move on. But, of course, he held his tongue.

"My congratulations, captain. It would appear that you win."

The Hawk's voice was conversational in tone. Not a trace of fear or even rage in it. Dusty grinned.

"Yeah," he nodded. "I'm funny that way. Get most of the breaks, don't I? Too bad you didn't figure that out months ago."

The Black smiled. Just a trifle sadly, it struck Dusty.

"The war is by no means over, Captain Ayres."

"For you it is, sweetheart!" Dusty snapped at him. "And just now that's plenty for me."

The other sighed, shrugged his shoulders and winced slightly from the pain.

"I wonder," he murmured softly, eyes narrowing to mere slits on either side of his long hooked nose. "Yes, I wonder very much. Perhaps, captain, you may be surprised."

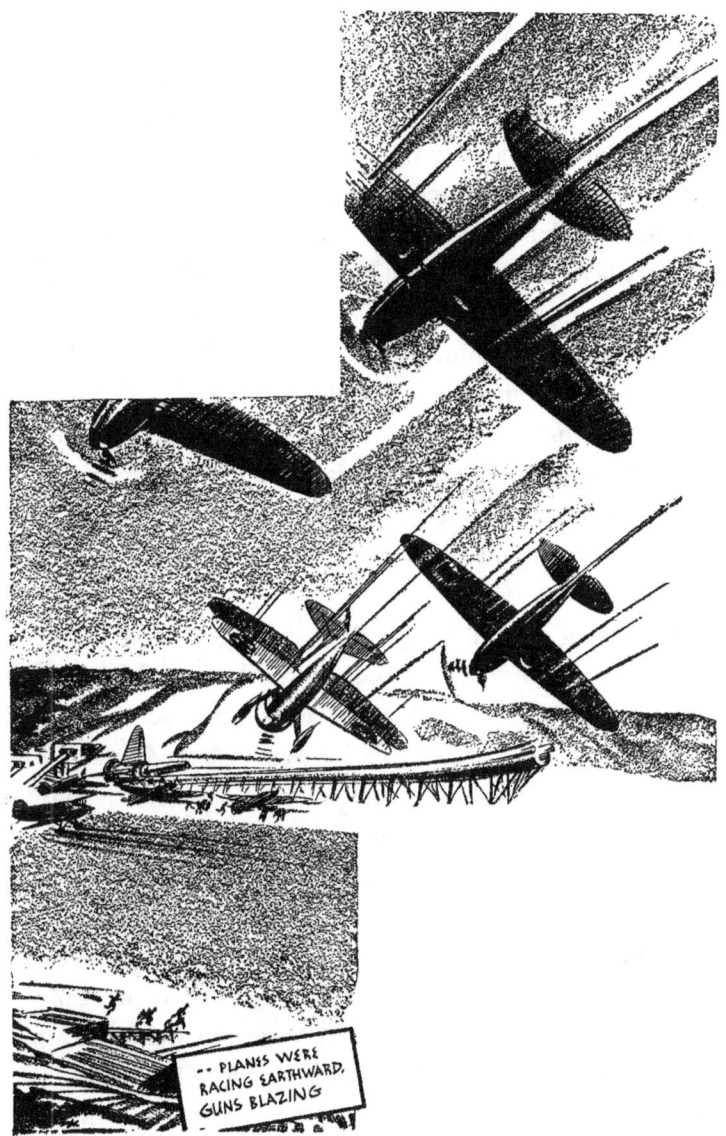

-- PLANES WERE RACING EARTHWARD, GUNS BLAZING

Dusty simply pulled down the corners of his mouth, at the same time arching his eyebrows, and said nothing. Horner and Bolton were half way across the billiard like field now. Another sixty yards or so and they would reach the nearest cabin plane.

Shooting a quick glance toward the mess building, Dusty stiffened and let the weight of his body sway forward on the balls of his feet. A Black pilot had come out of the mess building. He stood perfectly motionless, staring toward Horner and Bolton. In another moment two others joined him, and all three watched the two figures walking toward the line of planes.

Grimly Dusty brought up his gun, and tightened his finger about the trigger, ready to jerk it twice if the Blacks started across the field. Seconds that seemed like years dragged past. General Horner and Bolton reached the cabin plane, but the Blacks did not move.

"Get going Bolton! For goodness sake; get going!"

Dusty hardly heard the words as they hissed off his lips. To his left the Hawk still sat slouched against the back of the seat. In an abstract way, Dusty told himself that the Hawk didn't look so bad in General Horner's uniform. True, it was slightly tight about the waist, but not too tight. And then as he saw Horner and Bolton get into the plane and slap the cabin door shut, he breathed a long sigh of relief and gave his full attention to the Hawk. The words he spoke were like steel again steel.

"I'm still playing the game your way!" he clipped out. "I mean, you have often tried to fix it so that my gang would smack me, not knowing who I was. And so I'm going to let your lads do the same thing to you. On your feet, and get set! When that ship takes off you're going to do a little solo run out onto that field. And I'm going to run after you. Try and make that C.R.D. ship. Yeah, that's a good idea. I'll give you twenty-five yards start. If your gang or I don't get you before you reach it, then—you win. Come on—up on your feet!"

The Hawk remained motionless.

"And if I stay right where I am?" he grated.

Dusty shrugged.

"Suit yourself," he said. "I'm soft hearted enough to give you that one break—a twenty-five yard lead. But, if you don't want it, then I'll plug you right here and now. I mean it! Your number is up at last. I'd just as soon plug you right there in the chair. In fact, I'd love it!"

The Hawk's eyes blazed with stark rage, and the features of his ugly face twisted into a savage snarl. He fairly spat out the words.

"Then shoot, dog, shoot!" he roared. "The sound of just one shot, and my men will come and tear you to pieces!"

Dusty hesitated. And then memory of all the merciless and cruel deeds done by this man flooded back to him. He remembered, also, the countless times he had thought and dreamed of killing this war-snake in fair and square sky combat. Of how he had planned to meet him high above the clouds and crush out his rotten life with hot steel. But now—it had all turned out so different. A jerk of the trigger and the Black Hawk would be no more. His pinch-hitters might carry on in their own way, but their master would be dead—dead for all eternity!

The end of the trail at last—the end of a trail that had lead through the very pit of hell itself. A jerk of the trigger and the curtain on the final act came down. Hell, he couldn't do it. It would be slaughter. The Hawk was helpless—entirely at the mercy of his trigger-finger. He—Dusty cut off the rest with a curse.

"I hoped that it wouldn't be this way," he snarled at the Hawk. "I wanted it upstairs, my ship and guns against your ship and guns. But what I hoped and wanted doesn't matter a tinker's damn, now. One hundred and forty millions of my countrymen rate you a snake—a snake to be snuffed out at the first opportunity. And right now I'm thinking of their wishes, not mine. And besides, I don't go back on my word—even to a rat like you. So, Black Hawk, ace of a vulture brood, I'm sending you down into hell where you belong. Sending you down, now!"

Face marble, eyes agate, Dusty drew a bead on the Hawk's forehead, squarely between his eyes. He started to jerk the trigger and—stopped!

From high overhead came the whining howl of planes tearing down in a full power dive. Their roar seemed to virtually make the walls of the building tremble. And a split second later the furious chatter of yammering machine guns blended in with the roar.

In a flash Dusty half spun and leaped over to the open door, and glanced up. Two thousand feet above the crater, and slightly to the south six planes were racing earthward, all guns blazing. Five were jet-black monoplanes, but the sixth and leading plane was an all blue biplane, with H.S. Group 7 markings!

"Curly! Curly Brooks!"

160

The six planes were concentrating a deadly fire on the line of Black planes on the other side of the crater. The cabin job containing Horner and Bolton was already racing down the field in a takeoff run. And a ton of steel was slashing down at it.

One flash glance and Dusty tore into mad action. Forgetting the Hawk, still lounging in the chair, he whipped around, dashed over to the radio panel and slammed on full-volume power. In practically the same motion he snatched up the transmitter tube. His voice echoed and reechoed about the room as he bellowed into it.

"Curly! Curly—leave that ship alone—leave it alone. Horner—Horner taking off! Strafe building at western end. Strafe building at western end! Do you hear me?"

The speaker unit boomed out Curly Brooks' voice almost immediately.

"Sure! Where are you? Where are you? I'll land and pick you up!"

"Hell no!" Dusty roared back. "Strafe that building at the west end. I'm taking that C.R.D. ship! Don't let any of them out onto—"

He never finished the rest. In the excitement he had half turned his back to the Hawk as he roared into the transmitter tube. And in that split second the Black Hawk whirled into life. Like a flash he came out of the chair. His body catapulted across the room like a shell in mid-flight. Dusty sensed rather than saw him coming. He ducked and turned, trying to swing up his gun. But he was a split second too late and the Black

Hawk's body hit him with battering-ram force. The gun flew from his fingers, and went sailing across the room as he collapsed over backward and went crashing onto the floor.

The instant he hit he twisted his body sharply in an effort to roll clear of the Hawk slamming down on top of him. In a way he succeeded. The Hawk trying to twist with him, tried it a fraction of a second too late, and got his feet all tangled up with each other. The result was that he hit the floor to Dusty's left.

Like two rage inflamed tigers they both bounced up like rubber balls and lunged for each other.

"The way I wanted it!" Dusty choked out, and swung with all his might.

The Hawk hissed something in his native tongue, blocked the blow with his right shoulder, and bore in like a man gone stark mad. In the face of the terrific onslaught Dusty was forced to give ground. And as he did the Hawk's eyes blazed with berserk triumph, and his clenched fists plowed the air like piston heads. For perhaps a second or two he hardly realized that he was savagely fighting back. But suddenly, as his right fist crashed against something solid and a white hot dart of pain slid up his forearm, his brain seemed to clear as though by magic, and a mighty roar of battle gushed from his throat.

And then, as the savage yammer of machine-gun fire echoed in from outside, he went to work in earnest. Two chopping blows to the temple rocked the Hawk back on his heels. The man shook his head, snarled something, and backed up a foot or two. But Dusty was on him in a flash. A left smash caught the Hawk flush on the nose and blood gushed down over his lips and chin. A sledgehammer right buried itself in his chest, and his breath whistled eerily out of his lungs.

Cursing, shouting in the same breath, Dusty pounded and slammed the Hawk back foot by foot. Rage and fear lighted up the Black's face as he blindly fought back. A stunning surprise blow sent Dusty down on one knee and hand. Instantly the Hawk tried to lunge forward and crash him into the floor by the sheer downward plunging weight of his body. But with a movement faster than the eye could follow, Dusty hurled himself to the left and up. In the same motion he brought up his clenched right fist clear from the floor.

Too late the Hawk realized his mistake. A ball of steel fingers, backed by one hundred-and-eighty-five pounds of bone and muscle whammed into the side of his neck. Like an Olympic diver doing a one-and-a-half back-flip the Hawk rose clear of the floor, spun completely around while still in mid-air, and then went slamming out through the open door. His body hit the ramp and went bouncing downward.

So terrific had been Dusty's blow that the very momentum of his right fist and arm lunging upward threw him off balance. Desperately he tried to check himself, and failed. His right foot caught behind his left and he went sprawling on his face. Slightly dazed he lay blinking dully for a second or two. Just in front of him was something on the floor. It wasn't very big and it glistened dully. And then he realized the truth. It was the automatic that the Hawk had knocked from his hand when he made his whirlwind charge.

Sucking in his breath sharply, Dusty lunged up on hands and knees, scrambled forward and scooped up the gun. It had hardly nestled in the palm of his right hand when he was on his feet and bounding toward the open door.

"No you don't, rat!" he gasped hoarsely. "I said I'd plug you, and by God I will!"

But as he bounded through the door his heart shot down into his boots, and a yell of alarm spilled off his lips. Down at the bottom of the ramp the Hawk was jerking up onto his feet. In practically the same motion he turned and started running out onto the field—running straight for the C.R.D. plane!

Sight and action were one for Dusty. Like a shell leaving the muzzle of a gun, his body left the open doorway. Down the ramp he tore, gun out and crooked finger jerking the trigger. Whether he hit the Hawk, he could not tell, for suddenly, the Black swerved to the left and raced down the side of the field. Still on the ramp, Dusty could not shoot because the Hawk was more or less hidden behind the bottom row of buildings. And when Dusty reached the level of the field a couple of seconds later, the Hawk was a good hundred yards away.

Snarling a curse, Dusty half-spun and raced a dozen steps or more after the man, and then skidded to a jerky halt. The Black, who at first appeared to be running toward the mess building now being plastered with steel hail from the strafing planes above, was in reality charging blindly toward the row of three stratosphere balloons. In fact he had already reached the nearest one and was pulling his body in through the open port.

"The hell you will!" thundered Dusty, and at the same instant he wheeled on one foot and went pounding out toward the C.R.D. ship.

And when he was halfway there, Fate laughed and played its joker card.

A diving all-blue plane tore down and its pilot pumped steel at a racing figure in the uniform of the Black Invaders. From a long way off Dusty heard the clatter of those two guns, and even as steel hissed into the ground about him, some of it actually fanning his cheek with white heat as it zipped past, his brain did not immediately register what was taking place. Only when he instinctively glanced back up over his shoulder did the bitter truth slam home.

Feet still working like piston rods, he flung up his right hand and extended the second and third fingers, spread apart as far as they would go. And then in a jerky motion he moved his whole arm up and down.

"See it, Curly! Lord man, don't you see it?"

For one more second of hell the guns above him still clattered, and then they went silent. As the C.R.D. plane, mounted on its platform, was but a few feet away, Dusty didn't bother to look up. He simply sighed out in relief that Curly had recognized the mutual kidding signal, and practically hurled his body up onto the platform.

A glance proved that the cabin door must be on the other side. Ducking down he darted under the projecting cylindrical snout, straightened up and turned. The door was directly in front of him. And it was open. Through it he went, head first. And in the space of a couple of split seconds his eyes took in every detail of the interior of the cabin. It contained but a single bucket-seat, mounted forward just back of the center window. Fastened to the floor, one on either side, were two control sticks. And in front of them was a set of conventional rudder pedals. The control levers for the gas rocket power plant were attached to the center of an instrument panel mounted just under the center window. Flying instruments were on the left of the panel, and on the right there was a three inch throw-switch and a box-shaped rheostat unit above it. From the throw-switch and rheostat unit heavy insulated cables led down through a conduit that curved under the instrument panel and into the cylindrical nose of the craft.

Just a flash glance. That was all. And in the next instant Dusty had flung himself into the seat and was slapping down the gas rocket ignition-switch and opening the power control throttle. Instantly the entire craft began to tremble, and the throbbing of the gas rocket power-plant behind him pounded against his ears. Eyes glued to the dials he held his breath as the heat-indicator needle slowly slid around the graduated half-circle on the face of the dial. It was an inch from a red mark, and although his experience with rocket power plants had been limited, he knew that a take-off was impossible before the needle reached that red mark.

Cursing softly, he eased the throttle open a bit more. The craft shook like a leaf and started to slide slowly along the slotted take-off. But the needle was still half an inch from the red marking.

And then, as Dusty suddenly raised his eyes and looked out

through the cabin window, a bellow of rage gushed from his throat. There were only two stratosphere balloons on the field now. The third was a good thousand feet in the air and going higher like a streak of gray light. Two Black Darts and Curly Brooks' all-blue biplane were zooming up after it, guns spitting out streams of jetting flame. But the high altitude observation bag was leaving them far below, as though they were tied by cables to the ground.

A minute more and the stratosphere craft would be out of sight completely. Out of sight, and the Black Hawk inside its metal gondola safe from attack, and able to drift across the face of the earth and come down whenever, and wherever, it pleased him.

The very thought of the Black Hawk cheating death once again seemed to set Dusty's brain on fire. The needle was still a quarter of an inch from the red mark. With a berserk curse he reached for the control throttle.

"Take it, blast you!" he roared. "Take it and hold together!"

And with that he rammed the throttle open!

CHAPTER 13
STRATOSPHERE DUEL

WHAT HAPPENED in the next instant was really a conglomeration of things, all of which blended into almost lightninglike motion. Behind him the gas rocket power-plant thundered out a mighty throbbing blast of sound. Dusty's eardrums seemed to snap apart, and the inside of his head rang with the clang of four-alarm fire gongs. A crushing, driving force slammed him back against the seat. And for one hellish instant neither his feet nor his hands touched the controls. With a frantic effort he grabbed them again, and pulled slowly back on the control sticks. A ribbon of yellowish white, with a black line in the center was rushing toward him. In a half dazed way he realized that it was the take-off runway. But, in the next second it disappeared from view under the long cylindrical snout, and the craft went streaking up toward blue sky and white clouds.

Up, up it went. And then suddenly it whipped over on its side and went careening straight down toward the earth again. A wild shout burst from Dusty's lips, and for an instant he went numb with horror. The right control stick was pulled all the way back, and still the craft was hurtling crazily downward. Directly below, a Dart monoplane was curving sharply out from under. But it was too late—a mid-air crash was inevitable.

And then, like magic, the long nose of the C.R.D. ship swung upward and once more the plane tore for the sky. Two thousand feet higher the truth came home to Dusty. It was not the craft, but himself. Used to a single control stick, he had forgotten all about the one on the left. And as a result he had unconsciously put the craft into a beautiful half roll and a roaring dive earthward. Sheer luck, or perhaps the workings of his subconscious brain, had caused him to pull back the left control stick and thus check his mad dive down into crashing eternity.

Reaction from the close shave set his nerves quivering like so many fine-drawn wires.

A STREAM OF VIOLET FLAME ZIPPED OUT

But, presently, as his eyes focused on a tiny gray dot high above him he went rigid with excitement, and forgot all about jangled nerves or anything else. Up there was the Black Hawk— the real Black Hawk!

Letting go the right control stick for an instant, Dusty rammed the throttle forward the last inch, and then pulled back both sticks. Up went the long nose until it was but a few degrees from the vertical. Checking further motion, Dusty glued his eyes to the gray dot above and silently cursed the craft on to greater speed.

The C.R.D. ship seemed virtually to hurtle itself skyward. Yet, at the same time, for every thousand feet it streaked up the gray dot above soared up an equal number. Taking his eyes from it a moment, Dusty made sure that the cabin door was sealed, and that the windows were also. And then after a snap glance above, he let his eyes rest on the throw-switch and rheostat unit.

Impulsively he reached out his right hand and slapped the throw switch down. As he did there came sing-songy, whining sound from the rear end of the cylindrical snout. It was jerky and uneven at first, but in the matter of a minute or two it was continuous and uninterrupted—almost like a set of finely-tempered high speed gears turning over at the maximum revolutions.

He listened to it a minute longer, then with lips pressed to a thin line, he grabbed hold of the rheostat handle knob and swung it around to the first notch. Instantly the cabin was filled with hissing sound. The coils about the snout of the craft glowed a deep red and from the forward end a thread of white light leaped upward. Like a length of thin ribbon it curved and snaked skyward and then arced over and faded into oblivion.

Eyes fixed on the wavy ribbon of white, the edges of which blended off into a purple green; Dusty swung the handle to the second notch on the rheostat unit. As he did, the hissing sound increased in intensity, the ribbon grew broader, and it leaped higher into the sky. A grunt of satisfaction and Dusty swung the handle all the way back.

"Simple as that, eh?" he murmured. "Swell! Now to get near enough so that the metal bag will attract the stuff!"

But as he glanced upward again, he let out a gasp. The gray dot had disappeared completely. Haywire for the second, he slammed the craft into a crazy climbing turn and wildly searched the sky.

It was now a deep bluish black in color, and without looking at the altimeter dial he guessed that at least sixty-thousand feet of air space was underneath him. And then, he laughed harshly as he caught sight of the balloon again. The reason he had lost it was simple.

While he had been fooling with the C.R.D. unit, and not keeping his eyes upward, the Hawk had obviously found a stiff high altitude wind. Instantly taking advantage of it he had allowed the bag to stay at that altitude and had gone sweeping a good thirty miles eastward. In short, traveling in the exact opposite direction to the C.R.D. ship.

Sighting the balloon, which was now decidedly more than just a gray dot against the dark blue, Dusty swung his ship around and headed straight for it. But, a moment or two later he groaned aloud. The balloon had stopped sailing east and was shooting up higher again. In less than no time it became a gray dot again.

"Go as high as you damn well please!" Dusty grated between curses. "Yeah, as high as you damn well please. I can stick it out, too!"

But even though he spoke the words aloud, he knew in his heart that such was not true. The stratosphere balloon could stay aloft until the Hawk starved to death—after that, too. Whereas, his gas rocket power-plant was good for only twelve hours at the most. A glance at the power volume dials had convinced him that fact minutes ago. Nope, his only hope depended upon two things—both of which time alone would tell. One was the top ceiling possible for the C.R.D. ship. And the other was the skill of the Black Hawk as a stratosphere balloon pilot.

To answer either was impossible at the moment. The altimeter was of the usual standard type used on all types of planes. True, it was only graduated for seventy thousand feet. But that did not necessarily mean that seventy thousand was top ceiling for the craft. For one thing it was powered by rocket gas. And for a second, its wing surfaces were of ultrahigh lift design. That might mean that—

Dusty didn't bother about figuring what that might mean. At that instant his entire attention became centered on the balloon high above. It had suddenly grown in size, and as he stared at it he realized that it was getting bigger and bigger. Something had happened! The bag had perhaps sprung a leak.

Or maybe the Hawk was proving to be a washout as a pilot. At any rate, less than ten thousand feet of air-space separated them, and that was becoming less with every passing second. Eyes brittle, lips curled back in a hard smile, Dusty watched the ball gondola plunge down nearer and nearer. Instinctively he leveled off a bit, and set himself to reach out for the throw switch and rheostat handle knob. And then, without warning the entire cabin seemed to become ablaze with red light. Its dazzling brilliance blinded him for several seconds.

When at last he could see clearly again, the C.R.D. plane was hurtling earthward. Cursing, gasping he pulled the craft out of its mad dive and went thundering skyward. But, as he caught sight of the balloon again a startled cry rattled off his lips.

It was no more than five or six thousand feet above him and to his left. The main entrance port was open and the head and shoulders of a figure garbed in a strato-suit were half out of the port. In the figure's hands was a strange-looking object. At first it seemed like a length of bronze pipe to Dusty. But an instant later, as a stream of jetting violet flame zipped out from its end, he realized the terrible truth. The Hawk was shooting at him with an electro-ray rifle!

An electric-ray rifle! Never had he seen one, but many times had he read or heard about them. On the ground or close to any foreign electrical disturbance they were not of much use. But, high in the air they were most effective. Not from the standpoint of actually killing pilots, but for rendering igni-tion-equipped aircraft totally useless.

In short, the short-waves fired from the gun were of a strength to completely burn out all ignition coils and thus stop the engine of the aircraft. The balloon not containing any ignition equipment, there was no counter disturbance to effect the operation of the rifle.

And now, the Hawk, undoubtedly reluctant to continue to try and out-soar the C.R.D. ship, had made a surprise descent to melt the coils of the C.R.D. unit as well as kill the gas rocket engine.

Even as Dusty realized all that, he was flinging the C.R.D. craft around in a screaming split arc turn that finished up in a thundering zoom. Through glazed eyes he saw little wisps of smoke whipping back from the coils of wire about the long snout, and his heart skipped a beat.

Of far greater electro-magnetic attraction than the gas rocket ignition unit, the rays from the rifle had struck the C.R.D. unit coils. Contact had resulted in the blinding flash of red flame. Perhaps the unit was finished!

Above him the ball gondola was pivoting—pivoting around as the strato-suited figure tried to bring his electro-ray rifle to bear on him again.

Dusty groaned, kicked rudder pedal and sent the C.R.D. plane skidding off to the right.

"Oh God!" he breathed fiercely. "Make it good for just once!"

And with those words he swung the rheostat handle clear around the graduated half-circle.

Instantly the cabin was filled with an ear-splitting metallic scream. The craft seemed to be virtually ripping apart. Everything became bathed in an ocean of shimmering violet-white light. A great ribbon of it whipped off and up. Higher and higher it went. And then as though it had struck some invisible and impenetrable ceiling, it glanced off sharply to the right and smashed into the metal bag of the balloon.

Through a blur of ever-changing light Dusty saw darting tongues of greenish fire spew out in all directions. In the same instant the figure half out of the open port hurled itself clear. The electro-ray rifle was spinning down end over end.

Just a flash picture that registered on the retina of Dusty's eyes for an infinitesimal part of a second. And then a mighty, thunderous roar shook the heavens, and everything became blotted out by a great cloud of dazzling white. An invisible giant-hand smashed against the C.R.D. ship and sent it careening off into space. Dusty felt his body toppling over backwards, and tried desperately to hold himself in the seat. But he might just as well have tried to hold back a shell slamming out from the muzzle of a cannon.

Over and back he went like a bouncing ball. His head crashed into something hard, and a skyful of twinkling stars spun around before his smarting eyes.

Instinct forced him up on his hands and knees. Foot by foot he crawled forward, lurching from side to side. Controls free, the C.R.D. ship was spinning like a top. Whether down or up, he did not know.

Somehow he got his body back into the seat. Somehow he managed to grab hold of the controls and put them in neutral.

And somehow the terrific spinning stopped, and the C.R.D. ship came out of it in a screaming zoom—a screaming zoom straight up through a sea of sooty white smoke that mushed back against the cabin windows.

It took him a second or two to realize that the smoke came from the long snout of the craft. And a second or two more to become conscious of the fact that the ear-splitting metallic scream had died out, and that the only sound now was the throbbing exhaust of the gas rocket power-plant.

As he impulsively reached out and swung up the throw switch, and pulled the rheostat handle back to the zero mark, the smoke faded into oblivion, and he was able to see the snarl of half-melted coils practically soldered to the long snout which was now scorched a murky gray-black from the forward end all the way back to where it slanted up to the cabin window. Some of the twisted coils still glowed a dull red, but even that faded out as the wind rushing past cooled them off to a dirty bronze.

And then, as Dusty stared out past the nose of the craft, a shaky gasp of horror spilled off his lips.

Slithering earthward, like a shower of twisted and crumpled silver-colored leaves, was the remains of the stratosphere balloon bag and gondola. Not a single part of it was distinguishable. It was all like a waterfall of metal drops—metal raindrops that smoked and sparked as they rushed downward.

And in the center of the curtain of falling molten metal was the spinning torso of a human being. The head and legs were gone. Only the torso and the two arms remained. And as they spun downward they seemed actually to shrivel up in size, and to finally become engulfed in a small cloud of dirty gray smoke. Dusty swallowed, then stiffened, and his eyes became agate. "The end, rat!" he shouted wildly. "And with the compliments of the Twentieth Bombers!"

Tearing his eyes from the terrible sight, he banked the craft around and started sliding earthward. It was not until he reached twenty thousand that he was able to check his position. The result brought a startled gasp to his lips. According to his calculations he was a good two hundred miles south east of the C-56 area.

At the same instant he remembered that Curly and five other lads in Black ships were strafing the place the last time he'd seen them.

On impulse he leveled off and went slamming around toward C-56. But a moment or two later he jerked up straight in the seat and cursed. Hell, he could be of no help now. Partly damaged by the electric-ray rifle, the C.R.D. unit had melted itself apart when he gave it that one charge of full power. The thing was useless now. But if not entirely that, another charge would in all probability blast the ship itself apart.

"Damned if I'll quit, though!" He snarled aloud.

A sudden thought came to him. Reaching over to his left to the small radio panel, he snapped on full volume power and grabbed the transmitter tube.

"All American planes, attention!" he roared. "Go to C-56 at once! Emergency relief wanted. All American planes in range! Go to C-56 and help…!"

He didn't finish that either. The speaker unit suddenly emitted the excited, bellowing voice of Curly Brooks.

"Dusty! Dusty! Where in hell are you, kid? Are you all right?"

Dusty whooped with joy.

"Sure! Hell yes! But, you, Curly! C-56! Did you...?"

"And how!" the speaker unit cut him off. "The boys wouldn't play. So we just smashed up their crates on the ground. And a bombing unit finished the job. But, where are you? The rest landed at Rochester. But I'm...."

"See you at Rochester in half an hour!" Dusty roared back.

He had exaggerated the time, for in exactly twenty-three minutes, Dusty piled down from high altitude and leveled off for a landing on the Rochester military field. Below him he could make out five Black planes, and a Black cabin job—the one Bolton had taken off. But Curly's all-blue ship was nowhere to be seen.

For a moment fear gripped him. Had Curly run into trouble coming back? The damn fool! Flying solo over Black territory! He—

And then he saw Curly. His pal was in the air, and off to his right watching him. He heaved a mighty sigh of relief, and started to flatten out. But at that instant Curly's voice rasped out of the speaker unit.

"Hey, Dusty! That bottom wing—you'll crash!"

With a gulp Dusty rammed on power and went zooming up. Hell's bells, yes! The bottom vertical wing, of course! And the three-wheel retractable landing gear. God, dummy that he was, he would have piled up in a sweet crack-up in another minute.

Circling the field once he cranked up the vertical wing, and cranked down the wheels. And then easing the throttle back he gingerly slid down to a landing. It was far from perfect, but at least he came down right side up and didn't ground loop.

Hardly had he rolled to a stop, than a shouting crowd led by Curly Brooks, General Horner, and Agent 10 swooped down on him. Everyone was shooting questions in the same breath, and for several seconds no one got anywhere. Eventually though, Curly Brooks shouted the others down, and grabbed Dusty.

"Dusty!" he shouted. "The Hawk—was that—"

"It was," nodded Dusty. "And he's through. Now hold it! My time to ask questions. How the hell did you get there? And those lads with you—were they—"

The mile-wide grin on his pal's face stopped him. Brooks nodded at five pilots of H.S. Group 7 that made up part of the crowd pressing about.

"The boys and I figured something was up when you left," he said. "And we hankered to be in on it. But, we couldn't figure the picture just right, until Jack Horner here flew up last night. Then—well, hell, think we'd let you go a job like that alone?

"Nuts we would! So I tried to make the Blacks think you were headed for M-29, and in the meantime, just in case we ran into any of them on the way to C-56 I had the boys fly some captured Black ships. I flew my own so that you'd get the idea if you spotted us. But to the Blacks, I'd simply look like a captured pilot being forced north.

"As a matter of fact that's just how it worked out. We met three flights of them. But Jack buzzed them in their lingo over the radio with a fake yarn, and they didn't even get curious after that. It was a cinch all the way up there."

Dusty half nodded, and gave his pal the hard eye.

"Yeah, maybe," he grunted. "But perhaps I should smack you one, just on general principles. You damn near got me as I was running for that ship. And you damn near washed out Bolton and General Horner, too. Didn't I tell you—"

"Sure," grinned Curly non-plussed. "That was kind of close. But, hell, I squared it up, didn't I? If it hadn't been for me yelling at you a few minutes ago, we'd be pulling you out of that crate, there, in pieces!"

Dusty chuckled.

"Alright, forget it!" he said. "I guess there wasn't much danger, at that. You're such a rotten shot. But, anyway, you can buy me a drink for it, just the same."

He started to shoulder through the crowd, but stopped short as he caught sight of Sergeant Bolton for the first time. The non-com hugging the fringes of the group was all smiles. Dusty plowed over to him, and grabbed his arm.

"Guess I'm getting old, Bolton," he said, "and need protection now and then. How'd you like to hook up with H.S. Group 7 for active service?"

Bolton swallowed a couple of times.

"Gosh—gee—sure, skipper!" he managed to get out.

"Okay!" grinned Dusty. Then turning to General Horner, whose very attitude was one of a million unspoken questions:

"You can arrange that for me, sir?"

"Yes, yes, certainly!" said the Intelligence chief, bobbing his head up and down. "But listen, Ayres, the Hawk—how did you kill—"

"After the drink, sir, if you don't mind," Dusty stopped him. "The bum left a bad taste in my mouth."

POPULAR PUBLICATIONS
HERO PULPS

LOOK FOR MORE SOON!

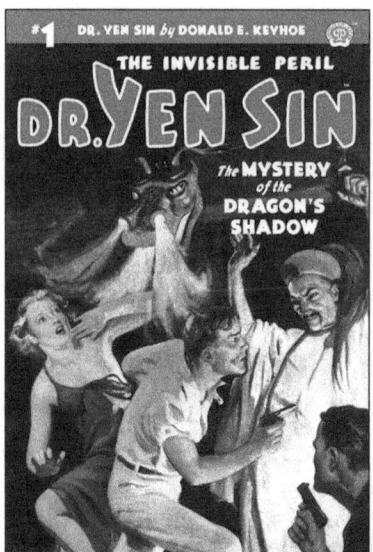

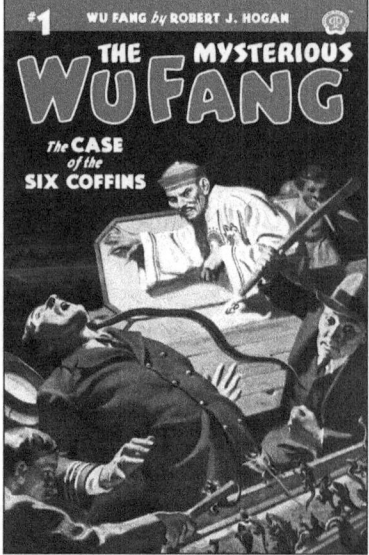